# Eagle's Nest

Scott McKissock

ISBN 979-8-89243-725-7 (paperback)
ISBN 979-8-89243-726-4 (digital)

Copyright © 2024 by Scott McKissock

All rights reserved. No part of this publication may be reproduced, distributed, or transmitted in any form or by any means, including photocopying, recording, or other electronic or mechanical methods without the prior written permission of the publisher. For permission requests, solicit the publisher via the address below.

Christian Faith Publishing
832 Park Avenue
Meadville, PA 16335
www.christianfaithpublishing.com

Printed in the United States of America

# Author's Note

As of this writing, I am seventy-two years old. You may ask, why now so late in life?

GOOD QUESTION.

Here is my best answer:

In 2018, a series of medical events evolved that changed my life. On February 18, 2018, I was admitted to the Cleveland Clinic Main Campus and underwent two successful surgeries for chronic osteomyelitis (deep bone infection) that saved my left leg from being amputated. I returned home to home health care, IV antibiotics, and twelve weeks of nonweight bearing. I was now confronted with extended immobility for at least three months.

I told myself, "You always wanted to write, now you have the time, so write." I scoured the Internet's numerous sites, each with its own game plan as to how to be a good writer. The prevalent common thread in the articles was, you need to write, write, and write every day. Three years and four manuscripts later, I finally stopped writing.

I had completed *Eagle's Nest*. My other future books will be *Madame President*, *Twisted*, and *McDonald and McDonald*—each of which is a love story existing in completely different environments.

*Madame President*. This talks about the deep state and corruption at the highest levels of American government and a female's climb to the presidency.

*Twisted*. This tells of the Chinese infiltration in American technology.

*McDonald and McDonald*. This talks about the deep state, power, money, and control.

## Chapter 1

For two generations, the McDonald family had paid their dues. They had calluses on their hands and arthritic backs from working the fields of the family farm in Crawford County, Pennsylvania. The one thousand acres spread, known as the Eagle's Nest, was the envy of every Crawford County farmer. William I and William II had done a magnificent job making the smart decisions, planting the right crops, borrowing at the right times and rates, knowing and talking to the right people, and being politically astute at the local, state, and national levels of decision-making. They were both graduates of Penn State University and were skilled at getting the most biomass per acre out of their land. Their biomass totals were the highest in the state.

The Eagle's Nest had diversified their business raising six hundred milk cows, six hundred beef cows, and raised grain and soybean as cash crops. The farm was the first in the state to have a functioning efficient methane generator. Eagle's Nest was a beacon for agriculture in Crawford County and the state of Pennsylvania.

Billy had been somewhat removed from Eagle's Nest the last five years. He was industrious, intelligent, imaginative, thorough, and hardworking, all traits of William I and II. He would, on occasion, unwind from the pressures of maintaining his 4.0 at Penn State by lighting up a Madonna one or two times a week. It was a modest consumption by any standard. Billy's best friend was Johnathan Best, a fellow student majoring in agricultural science. Johnathan's specialty was acreage productivity. It was Johnathan's job to figure out how to get the most crop production per acre. Billy and Johnathan met while enrolled in an introductory course in agricultural science and had been best friends ever since.

He was done with classes and his work for the week. Billy hit favorites on his cell phone and touched Johnathan's number.

Johnathan responded immediately, "What's up, Billy?"

"I was wondering how Nemo's sounds to you?"

"Sounds awesome. I'll see you there soon."

Johnathan arrived around three o'clock in the afternoon and had no issue finding their usual table. Nemo's is not a large bar and eatery but always busy. It was a perfect time to meet.

Jackie approached with a big smile. "How are you doing today, Johnathan?"

"Great, thanks. How about you?"

"Another day in paradise," she said with a smile. "What can I get you today?"

"I'll have today's craft beer special. Billy will be along shortly."

"How is Billy? I haven't seen him lately."

"He is doing great. He will be glad to see you."

Jackie was a beautiful girl. She looked amazing with her dark eyes and her dark hair tied above her head. She would be a fine catch for some lucky man. Jackie smiled and quickly returned with Johnathan's beer and went efficiently on her way to another table. Johnathan made short work of his cold beer and ordered another. Billy arrived around three thirty.

"Where have you been?"

"I had to finish up a few things before the weekend."

Jackie intervened, "Okay, boys, what'll it be?"

Johnathan replied, "More of the same for me."

Jackie looked at Billy and smiled. "What will it be, Billy?"

"I will have a Corona Light, please."

His polite response drew a huge smile.

Johnathan took a hit on his third sixteen-ounce craft and said, "You know, Billy, I've been thinking."

Billy was unsure where this was going, but he knew it would be out there.

"Billy, there is only a finite amount of grain that can be sustained on a one-acre plot. My three years of study at Penn State have been about squeezing the most biomass out of one acre of land. The average price that a farmer can get out of an acre of grain is $1,000 to $1,200 per acre. Even your methane generator at Eagle's Nest has finite limitations relating to biomass and methane production."

When Johnathan came up for air, Jackie happened to be walking by, and Billy ordered two more beers. He knew he would need another because he knew Johnathan was just getting started. They each finished their beer as Jackie delivered two more. Again, she seemed to give Billy a warm friendly smile. This time, a provocative tilt of the head went along with the smile.

His friend never noticed.

Johnathan continued, "Unless a farm has thousands of acres, biomass increases of 1 or 2 percent would hardly be recognizable in revenues. Much has already been done, and the next 1 or 2 percent increase will even be harder to achieve. In other words, cash crops are maxing out in terms of total possible biomass per acre. Costs will continue to go up year after year, and revenues will stagnate over time, unless there are major increases in the price of grains and soybeans. Your father and grandfather made smart moves diversifying their business. That is why they are successful today."

"Okay, Johnathan, what is your point? Cut to the chase."

They each took another sip of beer, and Johnathan continued, "Unless farmers get bigger, their chances of maintaining their present status quo will diminish significantly over time. Those present and future farmers who have their eyes and ears to the future must look to find a new cash crop. A cash crop that generates more than $1,000 per acre of biomass to keep up with costs."

Billy, being an agriculture business student, followed Johnathan easily.

"This new cash crop is marijuana. Billy, it is time for the next generation of the McDonald family to diversify."

"Interesting…Food for thought."

On that note, the conversation dwindled, and Johnathan decided to call it an early night. Johnathan got up to leave.

"Johnathan, I think I am going to stay, have one more, and take care of my messages and emails for the day. I'll catch you later."

"Later, Billy."

Shortly after Johnathan left Nemo's, Jackie stopped by his table and had a quick sit.

She asked Billy, "Will you walk me home? I will be done in fifteen minutes."

Billy responded to this unusual request, "Sure, I will gladly walk you back to your apartment."

Billy opted out of any more beer and began dealing with his messages and emails. She was gone as fast as she appeared, with a smile and a wave. Billy saw her pass several times as he waited for her to finish her shift. With every pass, there was a smile.

At 9:05 p.m., she approached Billy. "I am ready if you are."

They walked out of Nemo's, and Billy asked, "Where do you live, and why did you ask me to escort you home?"

"My roommate, Marlene, also works at Nemo's, and we usually work the same shift and leave together. She had to go home for the weekend. I know you and Johnathan, and you both are good people. I didn't want to walk home alone after dark."

That made sense to Billy.

The walk was warm and inviting, and Jackie continued to smile like she did all evening. It was an intriguing smile. The more they walked, the more Billy observed she was truly a beautiful woman. Their conversation was easy, and he was surprised when she grabbed his hand about five minutes into their walk. She said her hands were cold, and she would feel more comfortable if he would hold her hand. Billy held her hand, and it did feel cool but warmed quickly. They actually took a longer walking route as both were enjoying the evening, the company, and the conversation on the way to her apartment in the Lion's Den Complex.

Jackie had complete confidence in Billy as a gentleman. Jackie's instincts told her Billy was a good man, and as Billy would learn later, her instincts were never wrong. She invited Billy up to her apartment, and he graciously accepted. They went into her apartment still holding hands.

"Have a seat, and make yourself comfortable while I get showered. I want to get rid of the smell of the bar and kitchen and get comfortable."

She seemed to be gone for an extremely long period of time. When she returned thirty-five minutes later, he could see why. What a transformation! Jackie looked refreshed and beautiful. Her 5' 10" frame was covered with a loose-fitting light-colored nightgown that hung to midthigh. Her black hair was shining and no longer above her head. It hung loosely below her shoulders. Her thin gown easily exposed her perfectly sized and shaped breasts. A light-colored pair of panties were visible. To Billy, it all seemed somewhat unusual, but to Jackie, it was just getting cleaned up on a Friday night after work and getting comfortable. She loved to relax with a shower. She knew she would be safe with him. Her instincts told her so.

Jackie sat next to Billy, close but not too close. They talked about school, their families, their career paths, their faith, and many other topics. Neither of them touched or kissed the other. Billy was tempted to reach out to her but thought better of it. They had a great time and laughed often. Her outfit and appearance never seemed out of place after that. Jackie was pleased that they talked well into the morning. The more they talked, the more she could feel her body starting to inwardly yearn for Billy. This was the first time she ever felt this sensation coming from deep within her loins. Jackie was a virgin.

When Billy looked at the clock, it was three o'clock in the morning. He had lost track of time. In those five hours of sharing his life with this woman, they unknowingly formed a bond between them. It was a time of pure sharing between two souls.

Billy said, "I need to get going." To her surprise and his, she grabbed his hand as they both rose.

"Stay."

A rush of heat overcame her body. Before he could answer differently, she turned and led him into her bedroom. Billy knew she had not planned this part of the evening when she invited him up to her apartment five hours ago.

As Jackie and Billy stood there, still holding hands, Billy said to her, knowing he was about to be her first, "Are you sure you want to do this with me?"

Her response was quick and emphatic, "I am a twenty-three-year-old virgin, and I have never felt more comfortable around any man in my life. You are easy to talk to, funny, caring, kind, and you had several opportunities during this amazing evening to try to take advantage of me in this gown, and you remained a perfect gentleman. What else can a woman want? I have waited for this perfect night with a perfect man for a long time. I think the time is now, and I know you are the man. Yes, I want you, and yes, I want you right now."

Jackie knew her long wait was about to be over. There was no hesitation, and she appeared completely at ease with herself when she reached up and removed her panties and lifted her gown over her head, exposing her naked body in the dimly lit bedroom. She stood before him, smiling and naked. Billy was amazed at just how beautiful a woman she was.

He walked over to her to give her a light kiss on her lips and said, "Are you sure?" She nodded.

Her breasts were full and tight, not too large but definitely not to small, and her nipples were firm and enlarged in her aroused state. Her hips were perfectly shaped and met her waistline with artistic curves inward. Her legs were long and slender and met her triangular dark bush with similar beauty. Her face and hair glistened in the dimly lit room. She was the most beautiful woman Billy had ever seen.

She whispered into his ear, "Take me."

Jackie lifted and removed his shirt. This act was followed by removing any remaining clothing still on his body. Billy did not have to wait to be stripped to get hard; his manhood was already hard and enlarged to maximum size. He stepped back and viewed her amazing body as she viewed his. She looked directly into his eyes and smiled. Billy stepped in again, this time, putting his arms around her bare waist, pulled her toward him, and kissed her moist lips. The extent of Billy's manhood was pressing against her loins as she rotated her hips and pushed back. Anticipation was heavy in the air for both of them, and they could no longer put off the inevitable. She softly laid her soon-to-be lover onto her bed with his back down. She was now in charge.

Her body was beautiful, and her lovemaking was instinctive and pure. Their bodies and souls bonded that evening into a union of flesh and spirit. It would last a lifetime. When they finished, she cried quietly with joy. "Thank you for being gentle. It was everything I hoped it would be, Billy, and…more." She thanked Billy again and again.

He whispered into her ear, "It is I who should thank you."

She leaned forward, put her lips to his, and whispered, "Billy, I think I love you." He was instantly shocked. She continued whispering softly into his ear, exciting him more and more with each word spoken, wanting and encouraging Billy for more. She would not be denied. He had never spent so many beautiful hours talking to and loving such a woman. Maybe there was something special in this relationship? Time should tell.

As the sun came up, they awakened and began to talk about the uniqueness of the previous evening. How easy it was to talk to one another. What a beautiful walk they had.

How comfortable they felt with one another. The complete satisfaction and ecstasy of their mutual lovemaking and the special bond they both felt. Although it was Jackie's first time, her innate perfection in lovemaking far surpassed anything Billy thought humanly possible.

The sun continued to rise in the eastern sky. The rays of sunshine passed through the bedroom window and fell on Jackie's perfectly shaped breasts. Billy pointed this out to her, and she smiled. He began to kiss those rays of sunshine, and her nipples hardened, and so did his groin. Within a matter of seconds, they were again sharing their bodies so completely the bed rocked violently, and so did their souls, as they cried out in love for one another by name. They both knew what they had experienced for the third time was special. Although they were tired, and it was Jackie's first time, they each desired more. Jackie took the lead and climbed back on Billy and forced him deep into her body until they both gasped, and their bodies shook and quivered as Billy released within her for the fourth time. It was pure ecstasy for them both. They were a special couple. Jackie was a special girl.

They got up around 9:00 a.m. Both needed a shower, so they jumped in together and helped each other wash their bodies clean. They hugged and kissed one another in the shower in soothing tranquility for a half hour. It felt so right being close to Jackie. Neither of them were the least bit uncomfortable with one another or their exposed bodies. They then dried themselves in the bathroom and moved to the bedroom to get dressed, conversing back and forth the whole time. Jackie was pleased with her decision!

Billy walked into the living room. "I sure am starved."

"Me too. No wonder you're starved! You used a lot of energy last night and this morning."

"It takes a lot of energy to keep up with this special woman I walked home last night."

They smiled at each other as a glow came across their faces.

"Billy, do you believe in love at first sight?"

"I do now. You are the woman I have always dreamed of finding and loving for the rest of my life." Billy could not believe what he had just said, but deep in his soul, he knew it was true. Their bond would be forever. He drew her close to his chest and held her there for the longest time. Jackie remained in Billy's arms with her head buried in his chest.

She felt she had also found her soulmate and said, "Oh, Billy, I love you too!" When they separated, they made breakfast, and each pondered what the future held for the two of them.

## Chapter 2

As the leaves began to fall in Happy Valley, the days became shorter, the nights colder, and the football games more important. It was just a few days before Thanksgiving. Thanksgiving break would start November 23, 2018. The Nittany Lions' football game on Saturday, November 25, was to be played at Penn State. State College would be crowded. They would play Maryland. Billy wanted to get out of town early.

Johnathan had traditionally gone home for Thanksgiving with Billy. Johnathan only went home at Christmas. This year, Billy had invited Johnathan again. Billy's parents knew he was coming. Billy also invited Jackie, who was going to be a big surprise to everyone at Eagle's Nest. Billy wanted to surprise his grandparents and parents with Jackie, thus the secrecy. It did not take Johnathan long to get used to Jackie. She was a very talented and beautiful law student who loved his best friend. Johnathan also knew how much Billy loved Jackie.

It was amazing to Billy how much a female had to pack for a five-day visit. Billy packed all of Jackie's suitcases and travel bags in the back of his SUV. He put his lone travel bag and his one small suitcase in the back with Jackie's. Johnathan hung his travel bag on the hook by the rear window, and his bag went on the seat. They were on their way. Jackie in the front, and Johnathan in the rear. They pulled out of State College at 10:00 a.m., Wednesday.

The three and a half to four-hour trip to Crawford County began with Johnathan saying, "Billy, do you remember the night in

Nemo's when I made the argument for and the statement that it was again time for the McDonald family to diversify and add a much more profitable cash crop to their résumé? Do you also remember the cash crop? I suggested Cannabis."

"Sure, it was the same night Jackie asked me to walk her home."

She smiled and reached over and squeezed his hand.

"Have you given the idea any more thought?"

"No, not really, Johnathan, but this would be a great time to discuss it while in the presence of our legal adviser."

Johnathan continued, "As I said before, grains are going to get you $1,000 to $1,200 per acre for maximum biomass yield. An acre of Cannabis will generate approximately $1.1 million per acre with maximum biomass yield. It is becoming increasingly more difficult to squeeze more yield per acre of biomass in grains. Its future pricing looks stagnant at best."

Jackie interjected, "Billy, there are currently nine states, and the District of Columbia that, in one form or another, have legalized recreational Cannabis usage and many legalizing it for prescribed medical conditions. There is definitely a huge market for the product, and the market will only increase as demand increases. If we are to progress with the possibility of venturing into this tightly regulated business and maintain the profitability of Eagle's Nest, we will need to find a good biochemist who has a strong botany background. Billy can help with his agricultural business background, Johnathan with the maximizing of cannabis biomass per acre, and I can help on the legal end and schmoozing politicians with my personality and amazing body."

The boys just smiled. She knew she was hot!

"We need to become more political as a group if we decide to proceed. There will be numerous regulations on the state level and possibly on the federal level if Mr. Sessions has his way. I believe we need to begin finding out as much as possible about the states that have legalized and how their programs differ. What are their quality control mechanisms and their regulations governing importing weed into their state to meet demand? In conclusion, we also need to look into the long-term possibility of exporting the crop legally to other countries. Canada just recently legalized recreational marijuana. If all these options become legal, and we do not get involved somehow or someway, somebody else will. There, now I will be quiet the rest of the way."

"You sure are beautiful, smart, and sexy. I knew there had to be a reason I walked you home that night." Jackie responded with an accurate punch to Billy's right bicep.

Billy shouted, "Pee break," as he pulled into Sheetz just short of the Kittanning exit on PA422.

Having made the trip to State College several times, and having stopped here before, Billy knew the restrooms would be clean. Johnathan and Billy always stopped here for coffee and gas.

Johnathan asked, "Jackie, do you want anything to drink?"

"Yes, I would like a bottled water, please!"

She moved toward the restroom as Johnathan picked up the bottled water and two medium black coffees. Johnathan reached the register and paid for the water, coffee, and gas. Jackie returned from the restroom just as Johnathan finished paying. He turned and noticed how many heads turned as Jackie walked by. They all got in the car and officially clocked their pit stop at eleven minuets.

When they were back on the road, it was Billy who initiated the conversation. "I agree with both of you in your diagnosis of the situation, and it sounds like a logical step in diversification for the farm. The farm has one thousand acres. It has all the equipment and labor needed to plant and harvest the crop. I can see some costs in building greenhouses, transportation, security, building and supplying a state-of-the-art laboratory, just to name a few. We can meet when we get back to campus, get organized, do our research, and look for a qualified biochemist that fits our group and needs, then discuss the further feasibility of this plan. We need the facts, and if they have merit, we must do the toughest thing of all—explain this plan of ours to my grandparents and parents at an Eagle's Nest business meeting."

The SUV got silent but only for a second, and then the conversations continued. The Cannabis was not mentioned again until they returned to Penn State the following week. The closer they got to the farm, the quieter Jackie became. Billy could tell the pressure of meeting his family was upon her. He continued his conversations with Johnathan but left Jackie to her thoughts. The last thing he wanted to do was make her more nervous than she already was.

## Chapter 3

Billy's mom opened the door and gave her son a kiss on the cheek and a warm hug. Johnathan was next, and he also received a warm welcome from Mrs. McDonald. She then caught a glimpse of Jackie and asked, "Billy, who is this beautiful young lady?"

"This is my fiancée, Jackie Olson. I hope you don't mind me bringing her unannounced. I wanted to surprise you and Dad."

"Oh, Billy, she is beautiful." As she rushed toward Jackie, she threw her arms around her and gave her a big hug.

Jackie responded while returning the hug, "Mrs. McDonald, it is so nice to meet you."

"Please, Jackie, call me Milly. It appears we have much more to be thankful for this Thanksgiving." She observed Billy smiling with his arm around Jackie's waist. Milly was smiling from ear to ear.

"Mom, we need to get our stuff out of the SUV and into our rooms."

"Billy, you and Jackie can take the big bedroom at the top of the stairs, and, Johnathan, you take your usual."

"By the way, where is Dad?"

"He is checking on your grandfather."

The procession up the stairs to the bedrooms was repeated more than usual. Milly just smiled inside knowing the reason. She also took more than needed whenever she and Will went on a trip.

"I am planning dinner around six o'clock." It was heard by all as she disappeared into the kitchen.

Jackie took care of her clothes and freshened up. She said to Billy, "I think I will go down to the kitchen and see if I can give your mom a hand. Why don't you lie down and rest before dinner? I will be back to get you."

Jackie took off on her own to find the kitchen. She went down the stairs, turned right, walked down the hallway, and through the opening into the kitchen. Her instincts had served her well. As Jackie entered the huge kitchen, she saw Milly working at the island.

"Milly, is there anything I can do to help you?"

Milly turned and replied, "Bless you. I will get you an apron, and you can peel those potatoes in the sink."

"I would love to. Thanks for letting me help you."

Milly thought to herself, *This girl is a keeper!*

Jackie had started her assigned task and was just about finished when Billy's father walked in. He was 6'3" tall, blue eyes, sandy hair, glasses, jeans, flannel shirt, boots, and, she would bet, soft-spoken. Milly walked over to her husband and led him to Jackie.

"Will, this is Billy's fiancée. Her name is Jackie Olson. Billy wanted to surprise us with his beautiful girl."

After Will hugged and kissed his wife, he said, "Hi, my name is Will. I am Billy's father, and it is so nice to meet you. I am glad you are here to share Thanksgiving with us. Please feel welcome, and while you are here, what is ours is yours." He then walked over to Jackie and gave her a hug.

Jackie responded with, "It is so nice to meet you, Will, and thanks for your hospitality and opening your home to me."

Jackie noticed his voice. It was soft-spoken. Jackie prided herself on her instincts being right. It would serve her well in her chosen profession.

Jackie stayed in the kitchen and finished her task. Jackie and Milly got along splendidly, as Jackie told Milly many things about herself and her family. She told Milly she would graduate from Penn State with a law degree in the spring. In the remaining time, she told her new mom how much she loved her son. The longer she talked with Milly, she became reassured that her instincts were right about Billy the night she gave her heart, soul, and body to him in her first act of love. It would be the first of many nights filled with pure love. She looked for every opportunity to share herself with Billy, knowing full well he, too, needed her.

Dinner was great, and the evening was filled with conversation. Billy's parents were truly great people, and Jackie already felt their love for her. It was easy to see why Billy was such a good man and easy to talk to. When nine o'clock hit, everyone helped clear the table, take care of the dishes, and put everything away. A glass of wine was offered and accepted by all.

In the morning, Billy gave Johnathan and Jackie a tour of the farm. They each mounted their own four-wheeler and headed toward the cattle portion of the farm. The bovine portion of the farm served 600 Holsteins and 600 Black Angus. Those 1,200 cows also provided the energy to drive the methane gas production on the farm.

The grain-and-soybean-producing areas and their silos were at a different site. These two sites and the methane site all had paved roads leading to them. Each site had its own tractors and equipment specific for that site. Everything was neat, clean, organized, modern, and efficient. Johnathan and Jackie were amazed at the amount of land, cows, and equipment owned by the McDonald family. Johnathan and Jackie made mental notes and took pictures with their cell phones of items specifically related to the conversations in the car the previous day. Jackie also made a mental note of a large five-acre lake and a small cabin close to its edge.

They returned to the house at 11:00 a.m. Jackie was exposed to another round of introductions when Billy's grandparents arrived. William and Martha McDonald were wonderful. They both moved slowly, and one could tell they had experienced a long hard life building this farm. They, more than anyone, were responsible for making Eagle's Nest what it was today. They had both been slowed by the burdens of their tasks.

Jackie thought to herself, *It is essential to keep this dream alive.*

It was hard to believe, from what Jackie saw today, that these two men could have created such a beautiful farm and business in two short generations. She could sense a higher power was involved. She was amazed at the work and business sense required to pull off such a project. Jackie sensed a strong force when William and Martha walked into the house. She immediately felt this force penetrate her very being. It warmed her body and her soul.

The dinner conversation centered around the farm, with Jackie trying to satisfy her curiosity. One could tell she had a background in getting to the truth.

They were done eating when Jackie asked, "Why Eagle's Nest?"

Grandma Martha seemed to perk up. "When William and I were first married, and we started this farm, there was an eagle's nest in a tree not far from this house. William and I derived great pleasure watching the eagles in their nest. We seemed to form a spiritual bond with the eagles. One day, I decided to make a sign. It said Eagle's Nest Farm, and I placed it at the entrance to the farm. It has been Eagle's Nest Farm ever since."

Jackie replied, "What a great name! I love it! Are there eagles on the farm today?"

"We have not seen them for years," grandma replied with disappointment in her voice.

When Billy and Jackie slid under the covers on this Thanksgiving night, they were both exhausted and thankful for one another and a wonderful day. Jackie totally enjoyed Billy's family and learning some of the history of Eagle's Nest. Jackie asked Billy about the cottage and wanted to get away to have a picnic at the pond. They both were ready for sleep. Jackie whispered into Billy's ear, "I am so thankful for you. I love you." She smiled and drifted off.

## Chapter 4

Friday was a beautiful November day. There was lots of sunshine, and the temperature was climbing. It was going to be a great day for a picnic. Billy packed the basket with sandwiches, crackers, cheese, and wine. He placed the basket and blanket on the back of Jackie's four-wheeler and secured them with a tie-down. He had purchased some worms and minnows the night before and took two poles on their excursion.

They reached the pond around 1:00 p.m., and Jackie proceeded to set things up for their picnic. It was chilly but bearable. The temperature on the picnic shelter read sixty-eight degrees. A beautiful day for late November. When they were done, Billy and Jackie headed to the pond for some fishing. They were unsure when they left the farm if it was going to be warm enough for a picnic or fishing. It was a very productive day in both categories, with numerous bass and bluegill caught and released. Jackie caught the trophy, a sixteen-inch, three-pound bass. They washed their hands and opened a bottle of wine. They each had a glass under the beautiful Pennsylvania sky. When they were done with lunch and two more glasses of wine, Billy took Jackie by the hand, and they walked toward the cottage. Billy knew exactly why Jackie had asked about the pond and the cottage when they went to bed the previous evening. He hoped she would not be disappointed.

Billy embraced his future wife's body and laid her on top of him and began to kiss her passionately. Jackie responded in kind. She said, "Billy, how did you know what I was thinking last night?"

"Because I know you, and I know you always want to make me happy. Right now, I want you to listen closely."

Billy held Jackie tight and talked quietly into her ear, "Jackie, I love you. You are the most kind, loving, and caring person I know. You are beautiful, and my heart pounds whenever you are near. I also love your beautiful naked body and enjoy making love to you and the deep inward explosions of the love we share. You are so loved, and I want to be with you the rest of my life. I can no longer live without you." Billy became emotional when he felt several of Jackie's tears drop onto his cheek.

"Billy, I love you so completely. I can no longer live without you either." She kissed his cheek, and they both dozed off. When they woke, it was 4:00 p.m. They just lay there, completely silent for the next few minutes.

Billy finally whispered to Jackie, "Do you want to marry me?"

"Of course I do."

"Then let's pick a date."

Jackie and Billy sat up on the bed, gave each other a hug and a kiss, each grinning from ear to ear like a couple of children on Christmas morning. They discussed their options. They decided to get married Christmas Day. It was settled.

"We had better get back for supper. My parents will wonder what happened to us." They reluctantly loaded their gear back onto the four-wheelers and headed back to the house. Billy stopped his four-wheeler, and Jackie pulled up next to him.

"Do you want to tell your parents when we get back?"

"Let's tell them at dinner. It will be fun to see their reaction." They continued their trip back to the house feeling very warm inside about their decision.

When they arrived, Jackie said, "I will call my mom and dad tonight after we tell your parents."

"Sounds good!"

Upon entering, Milly told them, "Dinner would be later than usual. Plan on eating around 8:00 p.m."

"Is Johnathan aware of this plan?" asked Billy.

"Yes. I told him shortly after you left today. He took off on a four-wheeler and said he was going for a long ride".

"Mom, I think Jackie and I have enough time before dinner to get a shower, change our clothes, rest for a while, and come down and help you get dinner."

"Sounds good. See you guys then."

They ran up the stairs. Jackie arrived first and immediately went into the bathroom, turned on the shower, removed her clothes, and entered. The water was warm and felt good on her naked body.

Billy walked in. "You know your naked body is a weakness of mine?"

"Okay. We are on vacation. Come join me."

Billy quickly ditched his clothes and entered the shower. Billy pinned Jackie in the corner of the shower and took his woman, as requested, over and over until they were both completely exhausted and satisfied.

"I never dreamed that making love could be so beautiful, so exciting, so fulfilling, yet so calming." She kissed him one more time, told him that she loved him, and that he was a special man and lover. "Now let's get ready for supper."

From the other room, Jackie hollered, "I wish vacation would never end."

They had realized in the last three months that they both had evolved into amazing lovers and that they both were well equipped to provide each other with great satisfaction, and they called on one another to share their love as often as their schedules would allow. Jackie hoped she would have the opportunity to love her man one more time before they left Eagle's Nest and return to the demands of law school and making plans for their wedding. She loved the way her man could make her feel.

# Chapter 5

When Jackie walked into the bedroom, Billy could not believe his eyes. She looked magnificent. She was a goddess in human form. Her eyes were dark and sparkling; her face glowed when she smiled. Her long dark hair hung loosely off her shoulders and highlighted her dark eyes. She wore or needed little makeup as she was a naturally beautiful woman. Her dress was a light-blue cotton version, knee-length, a narrow black belt, dark-blue nylons, black high heels, and a simple strand of pearls. He looked at Jackie and smiled. She smiled back.

They exited their room at 8:00 p.m. When they reached the stairs, they heard Johnathan's door. They waited for him at the stairs.

When he saw Jackie, he gave his friend a wink. "Wow, you look extremely hot tonight."

She smiled. Johnathan said hi to Billy as they descended the stairway. When the three arrived in the kitchen, Jackie went to the apron drawer and removed three aprons. "These two gentlemen are here to help you, Milly."

"You two can place the tablecloth and set the table."

Before Jackie could put on her apron, Milly turned toward her. "You look absolutely stunning, my dear. You seem to be happy and have a glow about you."

"Thank you, Milly. Your son makes me very happy, and the glow comes from how much I love him."

This would not be the last time Jackie's glow would be seen and felt by the McDonald family. She was tying off her apron when Will walked into the kitchen and saw the boys working around the table.

"Milly, I have not seen this sight for a few years! What does this woman have over our son and Johnathan?"

She received her hug and kiss. "Whatever it is, we need to get it bottled and dispense when needed." They all laughed.

Billy walked into the kitchen and grabbed Jackie's hand. "Mom and Dad, Jackie and I love each other very much! We each care more about the other than we do ourselves. We want to spend the rest of our lives together. We love each other's company. We are going to get married over semester break, and we would like your permission to do it in this house, on Christmas Day?"

Milly spoke first, as usual, "Billy, I can see why you have been drawn to Jackie. She is a beautiful girl and a wonderful person. I can tell she loves you. Your father and I have fallen in love with her."

"Billy, your mother and I are very pleased with your choice. We will be honored to have Jackie as our new daughter." Will left the room and returned with a bottle of champagne. A toast was raised to Billy and Jackie, their lives, their marriage, and their love for one another.

\* \* \* \* \*

Billy awakened early, but Jackie encouraged him to go back to sleep and get some more rest. When he woke up again, it was 10:00 a.m. He stretched and noticed that Jackie was gone. He showered and headed downstairs. He could smell bacon cooking as he descended.

"Where is Jackie?" he asked his mom.

"Your dad and his future daughter went for a horse ride early this morning. I cooked us breakfast, and we ate together. I think they left the house around eight thirty this morning. I saw them talking last night before Jackie retired. Your dad told me last night they had arranged the ride. I think they wanted some time alone to get to know each other better."

Before Billy finished eating, he heard the horses running and then stopping near the back door. Jackie and Will were laughing when they entered the room. "This girl of yours knows her way around horses. She bridled and saddled Bullet. She rode Bullet like she had done it her whole life."

"I have ridden horses before. This was the first time in years, and it felt really good to ride again. Thanks for taking me for the ride, Mr. McDonald. It was a lot of fun, and I enjoyed the conversation and getting to know you better."

"You are very welcome, my dear. It was my pleasure."

Mr. McDonald always rode Bullet. Jackie scored major brownie points with Billy's dad that morning. Milly and Jackie exited to put the horses away. Milly knew Will wanted to talk to Billy in private and thought this would be a good time for their departure.

"Billy, I would like to meet you in the boardroom in two hours. You, your mother, myself, your grandparents, Mr. Moore—our accountant—and Mr. White—our lawyer—will all be there. This is a scheduled powwow, and since you are home, I would like you to be there. Billy, I also want you to bring Jackie and Johnathan."

"We will be there!"

As the result of his horse ride with his new daughter, Billy's father must have elevated her to family status. He apparently had also elevated Johnathan to the same. These sudden invitations to a family business meeting were curious to Billy, and it was extremely rare. He sensed something major was about to happen but had no idea what or when. Billy texted Jackie and Johnathan and asked them to be in his room by 12:00 p.m.

Jackie was back by 11:30 a.m., and Johnathan walked in at 11:55 a.m. and said, "What's up?"

"There is a business meeting today at one, and Dad wanted me to be there."

Johnathan stated the obvious, "This is not unusual. What's the big deal?"

"The big deal is he asked me to invite the two of you."

## Chapter 6

The boardroom was huge. There were pictures covering the walls with various stages of growth and expansion. The pictures were of different building projects, new pieces of equipment, the methane generator, and of William and Martha. The huge wooden table in the middle of the room was surrounded by twelve plush adjustable black leather chairs. The room looked more like the boardroom of a Fortune 500 company than of a farm in Crawford County, Pennsylvania. When Billy, Jackie, and Johnathan entered the room at 12:50 p.m., the other six participants were already seated. They moved to the open seats.

Will started the meeting by introducing Jackie and Johnathan to Mr. Moore and Mr. White. The meeting began with the minutes being read by Milly. They were approved. Will continued by asking Mr. Moore to read the treasurer's report. Jackie was amazed at how much revenue was generated by the farm. The total expenditures for the month took a huge chunk out of the revenues, but there was enough left over for everyone to live very comfortably. Billy asked Mr. Moore for the revenues in the grain portion of the farm over the last five years. In a matter of a minute, he had the numbers and projected them on the screen. Over the last five years, the numbers were pretty much constant at around $1,150 per acre.

"Mr. Moore, could I please see the cost of production per acre?" Within a minute, he again had the information on the screen. It was obvious that the cost of production had risen at a rate of 1.5 percent a year over the last five years, for a grand total of 7.5 percent.

"Unless Uncle Sam pays us to plant, we are losing money in the grain end of our business. I would like to thank you, Mr. Moore, for generating this information quickly and presenting it in a form that was easy for all to understand."

"You are quite welcome, Billy."

"Dad and Grandfather, do you care if Johnathan speaks today?" They both nodded in agreement.

"I would like to give you my evaluation of this predicament, and I hope I can do my job as well as Mr. Moore did his. My job as a student at Penn State is to come up with ways to gain or create more biomass per usable acre of land. With your costs increasing at 1.5 percent a year just to stay even, you must generate 7.5 percent more yield per acre over five years. In my opinion, that is difficult to do. Much has already been done in my field, and it is taking longer and longer to achieve smaller and smaller increases in biomass per acre.

"My solution is simple. Only grow the grain you can use in the bovine portion of your business or find a crop that will sell for more than $1,150 per biomass per acre. Every acre you grow that is not subsidized by the government is like burning your money."

"Thank you, Johnathan. We appreciate your expert analysis of the situation."

Will spoke with urgency as if he had something very important to divulge to the group. He seemed nervous. Billy sensed his father's nervousness. "Billy, we are especially glad that you came home and were available to sit in on this meeting because it affects you and, now, Jackie. Mr. White, I turn the meeting over to you."

"Billy, by the unanimous consent of the owners of Eagle's Nest Farm LLC, I hereby notify you and your wife-to-be, you both are the proud new owners of the Eagle's Nest Farm, including all the homes, buildings, machinery, equipment, livestock, land, savings, stocks, bonds, and all other assets, real or implied. You and your wife will be the owners of two prepaid life insurance policies in the amount of $2 million each. Finally, Billy and Jackie, you will be the owners of a $10-million trust from which your personal access is $3 million to use as you wish, $7 million to be used as needed in the continuation of this dream, and an operating account of $3 million. The total net worth of your inheritance equals $35 million.

"You two are very fortunate. Billy, your parents and grandparents were extremely hard workers and wise investors. Jackie, you, too, are fortunate. You have been given the trust of these two families and endowed with the responsibility to help carry on the tradition of Eagle's Nest. The document that I now give you contains the terms and conditions of acceptance. This contract, if you both so accept, must be signed on or before December 24, 2018, for it to be considered a legal document." Congratulations were offered, and all rose and left the three alone in that quiet, now mostly empty, boardroom.

Mr. Harry White and Mr. Steven Moore huddled at Mr. White's car. "Harry, what do you think of this transfer of money and power transpiring in that boardroom today?"

"They are incredibly young to take over such a large business. I also think that William and Will have made many good choices over the years and would not have done this just because its family. They did this feeling that this young couple was ready to lead this farm into the next generation."

\* \* \* \* \*

Johnathan finally spoke, "What the hell just happened here?"

The quiet continued until Billy spoke five minutes later.

"I think we just witnessed the transfer of power. I also think my family has evoked their complete faith, trust, and love in my wife-to-be. Jackie, honey, if you so choose, we are now multimillionaires." Jackie still had not moved or said a word since the meeting adjourned.

Johnathan said as he left, "I am going to take a four-wheeler ride and give you two time to comprehend what just happened here. Remember the Penn State game starts at 8:00 p.m. I know your mom expects us to be there. I believe she and Will are inviting a few close friends over for the festivities."

"Have a good ride, and we will see you then."

"Okay, I will see you two later."

It was 2:30 p.m. when they left the boardroom to return to the farmhouse. Jackie spoke for the first time, "Billy, please hold my hand. It is cold out."

They entered their room, and Jackie went into the bathroom. She said, "I need to get comfortable." She took a long shower. When she entered the bedroom, Billy noticed immediately that it was the same nightgown she had worn three months ago in her apartment. Billy, again, noticed her amazing breasts as she walked toward him, only this time, she wore no panties. Billy knew this was Jackie's way of relaxing, but the vision of her walking toward him was driving him crazy. She came over and sat on his bed. She sat close, but not too close. They began talking and sharing, and when they looked up, it was 5:30 p.m.

Billy said, "It is getting late, and I need to get going."

She reached across the bed and grabbed his hand and said, "Stay." They both knew what the other had just reenacted and smiled. They embraced.

She was up first and showered. Billy followed as Jackie started to get ready. Jackie sat in front of the mirror in the dressing room, combing her hair, dressed only in her panties. She thought about how much she loved her man. She continued to brush her hair. She thought, *I can't wait to marry this man that I love!*

Her thoughts were totally on Billy and how much she loved him. It finally hit her, deep in her soul, not once since they had returned to their room had she thought about the meeting or the millions of dollars she had just inherited. She thought only of Billy. She sighed deeply, got up from her chair, found her man, and gave him a loving kiss and returned to finish getting ready. He stepped into her dressing room.

"What was that?"

"That was a kiss!"

"Why?"

"Because I needed to give it to you." Jackie knew then and there, whatever they decided, it was okay as long as they had each other.

\* \* \* \* \*

It was Sunday morning, and all was well in the world. The Nittany Lions won their game with Maryland. The game ended late, but everyone was at the table and had already eaten their breakfast and drank coffee by eight thirty. Johnathan, being the gracious guest and knowing there was talking to be done, excused himself and exited via the back door.

Milly asked, "Jackie and Billy, do you have any questions about the contract given to you by Mr. White?"

"Mom, we have not even looked at it yet. Why now?"

"We are ready to take it easy and maybe travel some. We are very comfortable with you and Jackie leading this farm into the future. We had that agreement drawn up a year ago. When you brought Jackie home to us, and we saw your deep mutual love, your dad and I started thinking maybe now was the time. We immediately fell in love with Jackie. Your plans to get married and to do so in this house sealed the deal."

Will spoke next, "You need to have someone other than Jackie go over the legalities of this contract. Jackie, honey, I know you can do it, but it needs to be someone separated from the situation. You two then need to talk. You both have great potential in your own fields. It is important that you both commit to your decision, or it will come back to haunt you. Make a decision that best fits your lives!"

For the first time since the meeting, Jackie spoke to Will and Milly. They had been waiting for a comment from Jackie since yesterday. They were getting somewhat concerned. "Whatever we decide, thank you for your love! Thank you for your trust and faith in me! Thank you for your son. I love him very much! I am looking forward to having another mother and father to love in my life. I love you both."

She walked over and hugged Will and kissed him on the cheek. Milly began to cry and reached out to Jackie as she approached and gave her a hug. In that exact moment in time, the anxiety of turning over the reins of the farm to the next generation suddenly vanished. He knew Eagle's Nest and its wealth was now in the capable hands of his son and his beautiful lawyer wife. He loved them both.

## Chapter 7

The following week was extremely busy back at Penn State. All three were doing the extra work required at the end of a semester. It was both an exciting and busy time in their young lives, as they saw their educations winding down. Billy and Jackie also had a wedding to plan. It helped that Jackie's mom and dad were going to fly to Pennsylvania next week to meet Billy's parents to help them make plans.

Jackie punched the asterisk on her phone that called Billy and Johnathan. They both answered at the same time.

"Nemo's, one hour." And Jackie hit *end* on her phone.

The boys were there first. When Jackie walked in, they both rose to greet her. This was a result of good manners but also heartfelt respect for this very special woman. Billy left and returned with a gin and grapefruit for Jackie, and they began to relax and enjoy each other's company. They each had one more drink, and in a matter of an hour, they were gone to finish the many tasks needed done before the semester ended. The hour's respite was just what they needed to continue their day.

Upon leaving Nemo's, Jackie grabbed Billy's hand. "You know, this is the first I have seen you since we returned from Eagle's Nest. I need to relax for a couple of hours before I get started on my work. "What do you think?"

"I know how you relax."

They returned to Jackie's apartment, and she immediately entered the bathroom, turned on the shower, and removed all her clothing. Jackie quickly made short work of Billy's clothes and entered the shower. The hot water hit their bodies. They melted in each other's arms. It had been an emotional two weeks with no relief in sight. They continued to hold each other close, feeling the embrace of their partner. Billy was completely relaxed. Jackie held him close and gave him a kiss.

Jackie had never seen Billy behave like this. She had not even considered how hard the last two weeks might have been on her man. She continued to hold him tight, whispering her love sonnets into his ear. She finally told Billy she was going to put him in bed. Jackie grabbed a towel and dried off her lover's body. There was no resistance on his part, as she led her man to her bed, covered him with a sheet, kissed his lips, and rubbed his forehead ever so softly until he drifted into dreamland.

Jackie threw on a robe, found her book bag, and moved to her desk in her bedroom to start several hours of work she needed to get done over the weekend. The only time away from her desk was to walk over and check on Billy. She peeked at the clock in her room, and it was midnight. She had been working for six hours. Jackie removed her robe, slid under the covers, and put her arm over Billy. That was the last thing she remembered.

*****

Jackie was an early riser, and so was her mother. Billy was out like a light with no signs of revival. He had been sleeping for twelve hours. She needed to talk to her mother this weekend, and this seemed like the perfect time. She grabbed a cup of coffee and sat to make her call. They often called each other at 7:30 a.m. on Saturdays. When Jackie disconnected, it was 9:39 a.m.

She thought, *This has to be a record.*

She then called Milly's private cell phone number. "Good morning, Mom."

"Good morning, honey."

"I hope I'm not being too presumptuous."

"I have waited a lot of years to hear the word *mom*."

"That being the case, I will continue to call you Mom with love and pride every chance I get." Milly started to tear up. Jackie changed the subject. "Where is Will this morning?"

"Checking on his dad."

"Listen, Mom, I understand my parents are coming for two days next week. I talked to my mother this morning, and she knows everything I want. It is simple and mostly about flowers, colors, and food. Don't let her get carried away. Billy and I want this to be family and closest friends only. Our wedding party will be two. Johnathan will stand with Billy, and Marlene will stand with me. If there are any problems, just give me a call. Tell Will we love him. I love you, Mom."

"I love you, too, Jackie. Give Billy a hug for me."

"I will."

Things were starting to take shape up for the wedding. The only major item remaining on Jackie's wedding checklist was her dress. Jackie opened the calendar on her iPhone and thought, *We would be done with school on Wednesday, December 12, 2018. Billy and I are flying to my home in St. Louis, Missouri, Thursday, the thirteenth, for Christmas with my mom and dad. We would return to the Eagle's Nest together on December 17. My mom and dad would arrive on December 23. That would give me and Billy a week to finalize any remaining plans and hopefully find some time to relax together before the wedding.*

While she had her phone out, Jackie called Johnathan and told him about Billy and how long he had been sleeping.

"Jackie, he has had a lot on his mind lately."

"Johnathan, do you think he is okay?"

"Sure, just let him sleep."

"Can you make it over for pizza and beer tonight?"

"Can I bring a guest?"

"Sure, see you at seven."

"Okay."

"We may need your help to get through this, Johnathan."

"I know."

Johnathan arrived at seven with a beautiful friend by the name of Nivea Anderson. She was a beautiful girl that seemed to really be interested in Johnathan and vice versa. Billy had recovered and looked his usual self. Jackie was again her gracious, beautiful self, and Marlene was present to assist in any way she could. They each opened a beer, took a piece of pizza, and conversations erupted. It felt good to share this time with their closest friends, laughing and enjoying their company. Nivea explained that her research at the university was in plant biochemistry. Billy looked at Jackie and winked, and they both wondered if this unique pairing was coincidental or planned.

There was much to do tomorrow by all in attendance. The evening was cut short, and only Billy, Jackie, and Marlene remained at ten. Billy asked Marlene, "Do you care if I stayed the night with Jackie?"

"I don't care. I am going to bed. Good night."

Billy was still tired, and so was Jackie. They slid under the covers, held each other tight, kissed, and fell into a deep sleep in each other's arms.

Jackie was again up early, put on her robe, and sat at her desk. She figured she had about three hours of work and wanted to get it out of the way. She finished by nine and headed to the shower. The shower was short and efficient but not very relaxing. Billy had left around eight, and Jackie was on a mission to get everything on her list accomplished. She got dressed in jeans, a white blouse, and a heavy pullover Penn State sweatshirt.

She smelled coffee and walked into the kitchen to say good morning to her best friend, roommate, and maid of honor. "Thanks for making extra coffee." She poured a full cup.

"No problem."

"I know you are busy like everyone else. I appreciate you taking the time to go with me to the bridal shop this morning." Jackie walked over to Marlene, gave her a hug, and said, "I don't know what I would do without you."

They walked into the shop at eleven. It was Sunday, but the owner understood and made sure she was there for Jackie's private showing. They began to walk deeper into the store when neither knew what the other had done, and they simultaneously said, "That's it!"

It had taken a total of five minutes. They both continued to look but knew which dress she would choose. Jackie tried on her wedding dress, and it fit her perfectly. Her dress's reflection in the mirror was simple, elegant, chic, and accentuated her already stunning features. Perfect!

Marlene spoke excitedly, "Jackie, you look absolutely heavenly in that dress."

"Thanks, Marlene, I just love it. I can't believe we found one so quickly." Jackie's instincts told her that Billy would love it, and her instincts were never wrong. Marlene took a quick picture using Jackie's phone, and it was immediately received by both grandparents and parents. Jackie and Marlene smiled as her phone blew up.

She needed to do one more thing. She called, and it went to voicemail. "Billy, I found my dress. It is absolutely beautiful. Thank you. I love you, Billy!"

Jackie and Marlene spent the rest of the day together. Their first stop was to get a bite to eat. When they were seated, Jackie's watch read three thirty. They drank one drink too many, but it made for a much more enjoyable afternoon. Jackie was so happy that she had found the perfect dress she did not care if it was her only accomplishment of the day.

The last weeks of the semester went by too fast. Their finals and final projects had come and gone. Their final semester would be their internships.

# Chapter 8

They arrived at Eagle's Nest on December 17 as planned. The trip to Jackie's parents was enjoyable, but they both were excited to get back and help wherever they could with their wedding plans. Jackie's parents had fallen in love with Billy, much like Billy's parents had fallen in love with Jackie. Jackie's parents were happy with their daughter's choice of a husband.

They decided on the flight back home to not sweat the small stuff. With so few people involved, there was little chance of misunderstandings. A meeting at the dining room table concluded early, and everything was in pretty good shape for the big day. No invitations were given out, as Billy and Jackie were steadfast in their desire to keep it family only. This desire did not seem unusual to anybody that knew what had transpired over Thanksgiving.

The only people who were not in the boardroom attending the wedding would be Mr. and Mrs. Olson and Marlene. Jackie did not make them privy to the information. From Jackie's perspective, it was now strictly family business. It was now their family's business. What transpired in November in that boardroom was on a need-to-know basis, and they did not need to know now or maybe ever. Billy and Jackie remained steadfast in their desire to keep their new business situation as private as possible. Johnathan was also steadfast in his support of his best friends' wishes. Johnathan had become family in the eyes of the whole McDonald clan.

William and Will had been watching Jackie ever since the transfer of power and were impressed with the wisdom and savvy of the newest female member of their family. They also knew she would be ruthless and cunning in her efforts to protect her husband and the farm. Neither of the two eldest had ever seen a woman quite like Jackie. They both knew one thing for sure: Billy had found one special woman. With her by his side, they could accomplish anything. They loved Billy, but in one short month, they had grown to love and admire this woman who came into their lives and was the answer to everyone's prayers.

Before they left for St Louis to visit Jackie's parents, Billy and Jackie had asked Johnathan if he could show up on Wednesday at the farm. They would be back by then and wanted to meet with Mr. White and wanted Johnathan to be there. The meeting started at exactly at 1:00 p.m.

Jackie began, "Mr. White, I had this paperwork reviewed by my contract law professor at the university, and he said to pass on his congratulations to you for putting together a fine contract. Billy and Johnathan have reviewed it also. Billy and I will sign and date it now."

"Thank you."

Harry White also had Johnathan sign as a witness attesting to the signing.

"This contract is presently in effect, and all terms and condition thereof are now official. Congratulations, by your signing, you two have taken on an awesome responsibility to make sure the Eagle's Nest Farm continues for the next generation. I might add, you both are extremely wealthy." Mr. White departed. The room went quiet.

Finally, Johnathan said, "Wow, my best friends are millionaires."

Johnathan's comment broke the ice, and they all laughed at his comment as only best friends can do. "I am going for a ride on the four-wheeler and leave you two to your thoughts."

They walked slowly back toward the huge farmhouse as the snow began to fly. It was accompanied by a brisk Northwestern Pennsylvania wind. The forecast included up to four inches of snow between now and Christmas. It looked like they were going to have snow on the ground for Christmas and their wedding. Milly and Will were in the kitchen when they arrived. Billy told his parents that they had signed the papers. Billy and Jackie again expressed their gratitude.

Billy said to his parents, "Jackie and I want Johnathan on the payroll in the spring after we graduate and officially take over operations. If Johnathan accepts the position, he would be in charge of all operations at Eagle's Nest and answer only to Jackie and me."

"We agree. A wise choice."

Johnathan smiled and inwardly thought, *I will not let you down.*

Will and Milly were pleased that the farm would be receiving an infusion of three new Penn State graduates—two family and one almost family.

The sleeping arrangements had been determined by Milly. Jackie and Billy in the front upstairs bedroom. Johnathan and Marlene would be in adjoining upstairs bedrooms. They each had a door that led to a mutually shared bathroom. Jackie had already cleared these arrangements with Marlene and Johnathan. The Olsons would sleep in the secondary bedroom on the ground floor. When Jackie had cleared the arrangement with Marlene, she smiled and told Jackie it would be fine. She was excited by the fact that she would have easy access to Johnathan's room. She never told Jackie that she always liked Johnathan. This wedding would be the perfect opportunity to spend some time with Johnathan. Marlene knew she had to be smart about this if she were to be successful!

Thursday was going to be a fun day at the McDonald household. The whole house seemed alive and vibrant. Boxes filled with Christmas decorations were opened and lay in every room. Christmastime at the McDonald's house was a special time of the year. It would be especially so this year. Milly loved the Christmas season. She loved to make cookies with Christmas music playing in the background. When William and Martha walked in, and there were no decorations out of the boxes, she said, "You better get the show on the road, or Christmas will have come and gone, and we won't have any decorations."

"We were all waiting for you," said Milly.

"I'm here. Let's get going. Get the lead out." They all laughed, got up, and began to decorate. Jackie again felt a force which penetrated her very being when William and Martha entered the room. Her body warmed as if a spirit had entered her body.

With all seven helping and Milly being the commanding general in charge, it only took a couple hours to complete the inside decorations. Milly just loved having these young people in her house at Christmas. There was so much excitement and energy in the air with Christmas and the wedding. Will, Billy, and Johnathan assembled the pine and lights on the porch railing around the house. William supervised. When the boys came inside at 1:30 p.m., the girls had lunch ready, and they all ate together.

William said grace, "Thank you, God, for this family, these friends, and the love that we all share."

After lunch, the boys hopped into Will's truck and headed to Walker's Tree Farm in Edinboro, Pennsylvania, to pick up the McDonald family tree. Rick Walker knew what the McDonald's wanted and had it ready when they arrived. They had gotten their tree from him for years. One perfectly shaped nine-foot Douglas fir, bailed and ready to go. Rick and Will had been friends for years and traded favors many times during the years. Handshakes and Merry Christmases were exchanged between all, and they were on their way back to Eagle's Nest.

Marlene had texted Jackie on Wednesday and asked if she could come a couple days early. Jackie cleared it with everyone involved. Jackie called her back the same day, "Please come. It will give us some time together before the wedding, and my new parents can't wait to meet you."

Marlene arrived while the boys were gone. Johnathan gave her a hug when they returned and was glad she came early. Marlene looked stunning. Jackie and Marlene were of similar build. Marlene was two inches shorter and had blonde hair. Tight blue jeans and a somewhat-tight white blouse accentuated her body features. It was the first Johnathan had noticed just how attractive and beautiful Jackie's friend really was. He thought to himself, *How could I have missed that?*

Billy and Johnathan quickly got the stand and had the tree upright and straight within minutes. It would be left for later, when the two young couples could spend the evening together decorating the tree, enjoying each other's company, drink some wine, and relax together as friends. Dinner was early. The food and conversation was excellent. Both young and old enjoyed the evening laughing at funny stories. Time disappeared. It was 8:00 p.m. All with the exception of William and Martha got up from the table and began helping Milly. They were done, and everything was put away by 8:30 p.m.

Will and Milly took William home, and the best of friends moved to the huge living room to decorate the tree. Conversation was light, friendly, and enjoyable, and the four of them enjoyed a perfect evening together. They laughed, drank wine, and did a wonderful job on the tree. Christmas music played in the background.

Billy's parents returned around 10:00 p.m. They came into the living room and were thrilled with the job the kids had done on the tree. Milly thanked the kids for all their help throughout the day. They proceeded to give all the kids a hug as a further sign of their appreciation.

Jackie was last and whispered into each of their ears when hugs were exchanged, "I love you, Mom. I love you, Dad." Nothing else was spoken, but Will and Milly each glowed as parents would in seeing their newborn child for the first time.

It was midnight when they decided to retire for the evening. Jackie and Billy retired first. Johnathan and Marlene followed and were getting ready to go upstairs when Marlene suggested to Johnathan that she was not ready for bed. Marlene encouraged Johnathan to grab the wine bottle and two glasses. He grabbed the wine and glasses and followed Marlene's desirable silhouette up the stairs into her bedroom. They drank wine and talked until 2:00 a.m. They both desired one another and wanted to embrace, but Johnathan thought better of it, thanked Marlene for a great evening, kissed her on the cheek, and departed through the bathroom to his room.

They were both early risers. When Johnathan went into the bathroom with only a towel around him, he realized that the shower was running, and Marlene was in the shower. She was not the least bit shy as she turned to face him and wanted Johnathan to see what he was missing. She slowly stepped out of the shower, faced him, and slowly reached for a towel. She was his for the taking. He knew it, and so did she. Johnathan was instantly surprised by the sight of her beautiful naked body. He was impressed with Marlene's naked silhouette. It was hard for him to do what was right. It took him a moment to regroup, apologize, and return from whence he came.

It hit Johnathan—he had just made two great decisions: one last night, and one this morning. He could no longer just think of himself. He would soon be empowered by his two best friends to do everything in his power to protect Eagle's Nest, them, and their family. Johnathan would talk to Jackie today about what happened and get her advice before it happened again. He knew this was a possible line he did not want to cross.

Friday morning arrived as the sun hit the frost-covered branches. Johnathan and Billy put on some extra clothes, boots, gloves, hunting hat, and each grabbed a four-wheeler and headed to the bovine barns. They were going to meet with John Wilkinson, the foreman and operations director of the bovine area. By the time they had traversed the quarter-mile necessary to reach the holding buildings, they were already getting cold in the subzero weather. When they arrived, the outside temperature was three below. This was a massive responsibility, and they thought a great time to make a surprise visit and check on their man. Will was also going on the visit but would be coming later.

The girls decided they all wanted to see Jackie in her gown. They would all get in Milly's Tahoe and go to Martha's house so Martha and William could see Jackie's gown. Milly used her remote to start her SUV when she saw her windshield was frozen. Jackie grabbed her gown, and they were off. They had called Martha, and she was excited they included her in the unveiling. Milly, Martha, and William sat down, while Jackie and Marlene went into the bedroom.

Jackie put on her dress and shoes. She adjusted her hair slightly, and they both left the room holding hands. Jackie was exquisite in her dress. She was going to be a beautiful bride for Billy. When Milly, Martha, and Papa spotted Jackie, tears ran down their cheeks. Milly helped Grandma up at her request. She returned from her bedroom with a strand of beautiful pearls and asked Marlene to put them on Jackie. They were a beautiful set and accentuated her gown perfectly.

"Your grandfather put these pearls around my neck sixty years ago. We wanted to wait to tell you, but your grandfather and I were married sixty years ago come this December 25. We want you to wear them on your wedding day. We also want you to keep them as a keepsake to remind you of how much we love you."

Jackie immediately collapsed into the chair, overcome with emotion. "Oh, Grandma and Papa, I love you so much."

Billy's dad finally arrived as the boys were halfway done with their tour. A lot of their questions dealt with the cold, and rightly so. The outside temperature was three degrees below zero. All three men were satisfied with the tour and the man in charge of their cattle, all 1,200 of them. Johnathan realized if he was to take this job—and he would—he had much to learn, especially on the bovine side of the farm. He did not know the plans of Jackie and Billy, but he knew where he would be during spring break.

They all returned to the farmhouse at the same time. Marlene said she was going to her room and lie down for an hour. She asked Johnathan to come get her up if she wasn't back in an hour. Johnathan then pulled Jackie and Billy into Will's home office. He explained what did not happen last night and this morning. They both agreed that Johnathan should follow his heart. They had done so three months ago, and look at them now. Neither had a problem with them hooking up. Johnathan thought to himself, *If she was still willing and wanting him, why not?*

Jackie made note of Marlene's actions and behavior and that they appeared to be self-serving. Her instincts told her so, and her instincts were never wrong! Marlene did not know of their existing wealth, but she knew Johnathan was, in some way, tied deeply to this special, massive farm called Eagle's Nest. Marlene had just made a serious mistake in Jackie's eyes.

## Chapter 9

Jackie opened her eyes, put a gown over her naked body, and walked to the window. She realized, as she looked out the window, that it was her wedding day. There was a dusting of snow overnight that made everything look white for Christmas morning. Jackie looked in the distance and saw a pair of bald eagles soaring effortlessly. Although it was her wedding day, it was also Grandma and Papa's sixtieth anniversary. She remembered Grandma's story of the naming of the farm. The eagles had returned! Was it a sign or pure coincidence to see these stately birds in majestic flight on her wedding day?

Jackie walked over to the bed, lifted the covers, and looked at the man she would marry today. She spoke softly, almost a whisper, "My poor man, you have been neglected too long. You shall wait no longer. Your wife will take good care of you tonight and forever. I love you, Billy!"

Jackie got dressed and headed to the kitchen. It was 8:00 a.m., and the house was already alive with activity. Her dad, mom, Johnathan, Marlene, and Will and Milly were sitting around the table, drinking coffee and discussing what yet needed to be done. Johnathan and Marlene discussed getting up early and cleaning up as much as possible from last night's activities. They had followed through on their promise. They started getting the house ready at 5:00 a.m. The living room was perfectly clean and ready for the wedding. The white tablecloth had been removed, washed, dried, and put away. The tablecloth Milly wanted on the table was in place and ready for the caterers. Johnathan and Marlene had enjoyed each other as they worked together to get the house ready. The house, with the exception of the kitchen, was ready for the finishing touches to be completed by the mothers and maid of honor. The wedding was at 4:00 p.m. The same time as Grandma and Papa's sixty years ago.

The Olsons were slightly disappointed it was such a small wedding, but their daughter was insistent. The reason, they didn't know, but they loved her, and this was her wish. They knew their daughter was happy and loved Billy and this family. Their stay had been wonderful. The McDonalds treated them like royalty. In their minds, the Olsons had raised a princess, and she was to be shared with them and their son.

It was 10:00 a.m. and time for Billy to get up and showered. Jackie called his number, and his phone went off right where she had placed it—by his ear. "Good morning, babe. I think we get married today. For that to occur, you need to get up, get your shower, collect your stuff, and go to Johnathan's room. Billy, I will be in our room until the wedding starts."

At 3:55 p.m., Jackie descended the stairs to meet her father and Marlene. The photographer captured her descent. Her dad said, "Honey, you look radiant!"

He leaned in and kissed his beautiful daughter on her cheek. The photographer was in perfect position for the second memorable photo. At exactly 4:00 p.m., the processional was played and Marlene walked to the far end of the living room, where Billy and Johnathan were standing. As Jackie entered, everyone gasped at her radiant beauty. They seemed stunned by the beauty of this woman walking toward them. Billy was speechless. Mr. Olson held his daughter's hand and smiled at her and then her mother. Will and Milly were very proud of their new daughter.

Reverend Neal hesitated and then began. "Who gives this woman to marry this man?"

"Her mother and me."

Within ten minutes, Reverend Neal said, "I now pronounce you husband and wife. You may kiss your bride."

The service was exactly what Jackie had wanted—immediate family, their two closest friends, and no longer than fifteen minutes. Jackie walked right over to her mother and father and hugged and kissed them both. She said "Thank you. This is exactly what I wanted. I love you."

She then moved to Willi and Milly. "I love you both. Thank you both for sharing your son with me. I love him and will take very good care of him and this farm." She gave them each a hug and kiss and moved to Grandma and Papa.

"Thank you for the pearls. They are beautiful. I know that you two worked very hard to create this farm. I want to assure you I love your grandson. I will work with him tirelessly to preserve what you have created. I will use every tool in my arsenal to keep and grow this farm. God bless you two. I love you very much." She then gave them each a hug and kiss, and the force she felt twice before immediately penetrated her body and soul. She felt warm, and her blood felt as if it would boil.

By the time they were finished, and the doors were slid back into the walls separating the dining room from the living room, the caterers had already moved in and organized the dining room and kitchen, and dinner was served. Toasts were made and champagne drank. At 8:00 p.m., the new couple was out the door and on their way to Peak and Peak Resort. It was about an hour's drive from the farm. Jackie wanted to stay relatively close, and this was the perfect spot. They reserved a room for three nights. It had a fireplace, hot tub, and large bed. The roads were not bad, and the snow had stopped. They arrived at 9:30 p.m.

When they entered their room, music was playing softly, the fireplace was burning, hot-tub lights were on, and on the small table next to the hot tube was a bottle of champagne, two glasses, and a bowl of strawberries. The room was perfect for love. Jackie was standing by the fireplace as Billy came close. She grabbed him and pulled him close and kissed him.

"You have been so kind and patient the last two weeks. I am here now and am going to take care of you night and day for three days. Whatever you could possibly desire is yours." The evening and the remainder of their stay was filled with passion and love. They were totally immersed in each other. They enjoyed their evening walkabouts, holding each other's hand, lying in bed together, enjoying the presence of the other, the quiet talk shared as they ate their meals, and their talks that lasted long into the night while sipping wine and enjoying the fire. Most of all, they enjoyed sharing and giving themselves to one another as husband and wife.

Her commitment to remaining a virgin was finally unlocked by this loving man not more than three months earlier. Her instincts were right about him. On this Christmas Day, when she said I do, she again made a commitment to this same man to love him forever. Jackie Olson McDonald would do anything for her man. She knew he would love her, take care of her, and respect her forever. Her instincts told her so, and her instincts were never wrong. Jackie Olson McDonald figured that this man demanded and deserved her complete love and her complete respect for the rest of her life. She intended to make it so!

## Chapter 10

They returned home to Eagle's Nest on Saturday, December 29, around 2:00 p.m., and spent the rest of the day and evening sharing with their family. They spent several hours discussing the wedding and reception and how beautiful it and the bride were. Jackie told Milly about their relaxing meals and walkabouts they took every evening. They discussed the room and its amenities.

"Mom, it was just so nice to get away and spend every second together. We talked and shared so many things. I love him so much."

Billy told them of their plans to contact their advisers and get their internships changed to Eagle's Nest. They informed their parents that Johnathan was going to do the same. They requested and received permission for all three of them to live in the farmhouse since communication was going to be critical between the three of them and Jackie's new mom and dad. They also asked if they would mind opening their house to a friend of Johnathan's for two days, during New Year's Eve and Day. They received permission, and they both thanked their parents. Jackie reminded them that all six McDonalds had a meeting on January 3, at 1:00 p.m., with the accountant.

Johnathan and Nivea arrived around 4:00 p.m. for a traditional pork and sauerkraut New Year's Eve dinner in the McDonald household. Nivea was glad to see everyone again. She immediately thanked Will and Milly for their hospitality and for opening their home to her. She looked beautiful to Johnathan and to everyone else at the dinner table. They spent most of the evening talking and getting to know more about this beautiful girl who seemed to be interested in Johnathan. At midnight, they all raised their glasses and wished everyone a happy New Year. Shortly thereafter, everyone retired.

Johnathan had just gotten comfortable in his room when he heard a very quiet knock on his bathroom door. Nivea pushed open the door slightly and saw Johnathan in his boxers. "May I come in, Johnathan?"

"Sure."

"I am lonely and would like to talk."

They walked to the bed and sat with their legs crossed.

"Are you uncomfortable with my appearance?" Nivea's nightie was thin with no bra underneath.

"Yes, I am just fine with the way you look right now."

"Why have you not tried to make love to me, Johnathan? Many other men have tried without success."

"Because I think I love you and respect you, your wishes, and your body."

"Johnathan, you are a good man. I love you. I promise, someday soon, I will make you a very happy man."

They wrapped themselves in each other's arms and found themselves in the same position in the morning. They showered together, got dressed, and came down the stairs together. Billy and Jackie were waiting for them. They all smiled and said good morning to one another. Jackie had made pancakes, and Billy made the sausage and eggs. They all started eating and talking. Shortly thereafter, Will and Milly arrived, and they joined in the party. Jackie felt that something was different. Her instincts told her it was good.

The meeting scheduled for January 3, 2019, started at 1:00 p.m. sharp.

In attendance were the McDonalds, Johnathan, Mr. White, and Mr. Moore. Billy and Jackie were now sitting at the head of the table, signifying the legal change in power within the family.

Billy spoke, "Mr. Moore, you may proceed."

"I have just passed out a complete financial breakdown of Eagle's Nest. It is accurate, and to a trained eye, it will tell much about the long-term sustainability of this farm."

Jackie interjected, "Mr. Moore, in your opinion, what is the biggest concern about the financial sustainability of this farm into the future?"

"Overall, it is excellent. In reviewing this document, I have found the weakest area for continued growth and profit to be in the grain production. This was so accurately and thoroughly described by Mr. Johnathan Best at our last meeting. I feel that his suggestion to begin the research to find a cash crop that will generate more than $1,200 per acre of biomass is the prudent place to start."

"Thank you, Mr. Moore. I would like to have the authority to consider oil and gas exploration on the property."

Mr. White interjected, "Billy, you and your wife have already been given the authority. Mr. and Mrs. William McDonald III, you have the complete authority."

Jackie stood and spoke, "I would like to thank Johnathan. He had made this discovery at school and warned Billy and me of this potential problem long before we came into power. Johnathan, you are a true and trusted friend of this family. Thank you!"

Jackie concluded, "Dear God, bless my husband, this family, these friends, and this farm. Amen. Adjourned." Jackie had just stated a new tradition at the McDonald business meetings.

Jackie and Billy decided to take Grandma and Papa home. They got them safely in the house and stayed to visit. Papa said, "You kids are doing a wonderful job. You may be the best McDonalds to ever run this farm." Grandma gave them both a piece of warm apple pie with ice cream. Grandma Martha pulled Jackie to the side before they left and thanked her for starting the new tradition of a prayer at the end of their meetings.

"Papa and I love you so much. You have been the answer to our prayers. Your papa and I can now pass knowing that you and Billy will take care of us, even in death." Jackie knew her reference immediately.

She smiled at Grandma Martha as she felt the force and said, "Yes, we will." A feeling of warmth overcame Jackie as she spoke.

On the way home, Jackie asked, "Billy, what did you think of our meeting?"

"I thought it went good. I guess it took the comment from Mr. White for me to finally realize that we are really in charge. What do you think about talking to Johnathan and seeing if he is in favor of getting Nivea here on site to do her internship?"

Jackie paused and thought, "I think at this point, no harm no foul. If it's okay with Johnathan, and if your dad is willing to write the letter, then it is solely her decision?"

"I agree. We are too early into this to make a final decision on her. We need to see where this goes with her and Johnathan and get to know her better. Jackie, we need to get my dad's opinion on this ASAP."

"I know. Timing is everything!"

As they entered the kitchen, Will said, "Thanks for taking Mom and Dad home."

"No problem. We love to spend time with them whenever we can. Do they seem like they are slipping?"

Will spoke again, "I have noticed them both getting worse in the last six months. I am glad they had the opportunity to meet you and go to the wedding."

"Me too."

## Chapter 11

The meeting scheduled for Wednesday, January 10, 2019, began at exactly 1:00 p.m.

All the McDonalds were present. Mr. White, Mr. Moore, and Johnathan were also present. Billy and Jackie stood together, and Jackie began to speak, "All four of the internships have been approved by the university. Starting immediately, Billy, Johnathan, Nivea, and myself will now be located here at the farm, finishing our degree work. This will allow us to actively get involved with the farm and its operation. Nivea, a plant biochemist, will be joining us tomorrow morning."

White and Moore were sufficiently impressed at how quickly things were happening.

"The next order of business relates to our meeting on Wednesday, January 3, 2018. Billy and I are about to pursue the possibility of diversifying into another business which, when paired with what is already present, will make this farm the most unique farming environment in all of the United States and, possibly, the world."

William sat up in his chair and started to focus on what was about to be presented. He realized that he could possibly be seeing the future of Eagle's Nest before his eyes. His prayers were again being answered by this beautiful woman who called him Papa.

Billy looked at Jackie and smiled. She continued, "We have been focusing on this problem of reaching biomass potential with little or no reasonable increase per acre in the near or distant future. We have searched and searched for a crop that could replace our present options. We found a crop that is in legal demand, and the demand is increasing daily. If we do not pursue this option, somebody else will, and we will have missed an opportunity. This crop can generate 1.1 million in biomass per acre."

Grandpa stood up and said out loud, "I'll be damned! It's marijuana! Pure genius."

On that note, Jackie requested that they meet in two weeks, January 24, 2019, at 1:00 p.m. Ideas and concerns would be welcomed from all.

Jackie looked at Billy, smiled, and whispered, "Timing is everything."

Jackie closed the meeting, "God bless my husband, our family, our friends, and this farm. Amen. Adjourned."

The two oldest statesmen left together. Will said, "Interesting idea."

The other McDonald, William, said as he left, shaking his head, "It's pure genius."

Billy, Jackie, and Johnathan looked at each other and smiled. They could see why this farm had been so successful.

The four interns would meet in the boardroom tomorrow morning at 8:00 a.m. Nivea would join them when she arrived. They had a lot of work to do. Billy and Jackie walked out of the boardroom hand in hand and decided they needed a walkabout. They returned to the farmhouse two hours later, and Johnathan and Nivea were in the living room brainstorming ideas for the laboratory. Billy and Jackie welcomed Nivea, and headed up to their room.

All four had their own separate responsibilities to the university and also to Will as part of their internship at Eagle's Nest. Jackie also had two days of service a week to Mr. White. He knew there were going to be many legal ramifications as this energetic group organized their plan of attack. His only requirement of Jackie was a two-page summary every week. His interest in this project was piqued, and he wanted to review it weekly by reading her summary.

Billy started the meeting off by reinforcing, first and foremost, "We have a one-thousand-acre farm to run here. We have to do it better than it was done yesterday and the day before and the day before. Keep your eye on the ball. Secondly, we all are working for the Eagle's Nest Farm as far as the university is concerned and as far as my dad is concerned. He has agreed to pay you $250 a week, plus room and board. We will be responsible for our own cooking and any cleaning in the kitchen. We will also be responsible for our laundry and keeping the upstairs spotless. We will meet in the kitchen every morning at 6:30 a.m. and be in the boardroom by 8:00 a.m. We need to work together to get the farm's work done and still have enough time to work on our feasibility study for the new cash crop and our internship requirements. Saturday is a workday. Sunday, use as you wish.

"Johnathan and Nivea, you guys are a team and can work together evaluating and improving both sides of the farm. Your areas of expertise complement one another. Once you get organized, pull in the foreman and pick their brains. They are there every day. Johnathan, you can fill in Nivea on our new area of research. I would like you guys to put together an early progress report on what you think Nivea would need in a laboratory building and equipment to be used in all aspects of our business. I want it on the twenty-fourth."

Johnathan and Nivea got on a four-wheeler, and Johnathan gave Nivea a complete tour of the farm. They made several stops, introducing Nivea to the two foreman and employees on both sides of the farm.

When Nivea saw the cottage by the lake, she told Johnathan, "I want to see the inside. Johnathan, can we turn on the heat? It is cold in here!" Within minutes, they had to shed some of their clothes.

"Johnathan, today is the day I make you a happy man."

"Nivea, today is the day I make you a happy woman."

\* \* \* \* \*

They were back on their four-wheeler within an hour, each anticipating the evening. Billy and Jackie were still at the table when Team Johnathan returned. Jackie told them, "You guys can use the table to spread out and get organized. We are going for a walkabout." They left holding hands as usual.

Johnathan told Nivea, "They love to take these walks and talk about their lives together. I have never met a couple, young or old, that love each other as much as they do."

Milly called Johnathan around 5:00 p.m. "I cooked roast beef, potatoes, carrots, and cherry pie. It will be ready at 6:00 p.m. Billy is not answering his phone."

"They are on one of their famous walkabouts, and they probably shut off their phones."

"If they get back, let them know dinner is at 6:00 p.m."

"Okay, Mrs. McDonald."

They were almost back to the farm when Jackie looked at Billy. "If this project is not feasible, or for some unknown reason, it does not fly, I want to get pregnant and have our baby. My clock is ticking, Billy." Billy wrapped his arms around his wife and held her for five minutes. He kissed her on the cheek and told her he loved her as they moved toward the farm.

Billy told Jackie, "I would like that too."

They entered the kitchen to find two plates sitting at the counter. It looked good, and they were both starved. While they ate, Team Johnathan finish the dishes and wiped down all of the countertop. Will and Milly came back to the kitchen to talk to the young people and have a cup of coffee. Everyone headed to their bedrooms as good nights were exchanged.

The night was full of love in the Eagle's Nest. Johnathan and Nivea consummated the loss of her virginity several times. Someday soon had come to Johnathan as Nivea made him a very happy man.

The conversation of having Billy's baby stirred inside Jackie. With each step she climbed, she wanted her man more and more. "Billy, I want you really bad tonight, maybe more than ever."

"I want you too."

Jackie and Billy had become masterful lovers, each with the tools and the desire to completely satisfy the other. Their love was powerful and strong and could be repeated. What occurred that night was sensuous, gentle, and loving. Their sexual experience that night lasted into the early morning. How they used their bodies to satisfy the other and their immeasurable desire and love for one another was a gift from God.

All four interns were at the table at 6:30 a.m. Jackie looked absolutely stunning. Her eyes were sparkling and her face slightly flushed. Her black hair hung off her shoulders in perfect position. Billy thought she had to be a caterpillar and metamorphically transformed herself at night into this beautiful butterfly that emerged every morning from her cocoon, more beautiful than the day before. He thought to himself, *I am truly a lucky man.*

## Chapter 12

The days came and went with all four putting in long hours and working very hard to keep the farm running at peak efficiency and researching their project at the same time. It was 6:15 a.m., a beautiful morning with the temperature in the teens and the forecast calling for sun. The interns were joined by Will this morning for breakfast. He often joined them in the morning. It seemed the best time to talk to his interns. He had a responsibility to these young adults and to the university; he wanted to fulfill it as professionally as possible.

It was Wednesday, January 24, 2019, and they were excitedly looking forward to making their presentations at today's board meeting. The talk around the table was continuous. You could hear and feel the excitement in their voices as they discussed what still needed done. They finished, cleaned up their mess, and headed to the boardroom.

Will told them, "Good luck." They departed through the back door.

Today Grandma and Papa were in attendance, and they both looked like they were moving with more energy in their gait as they came into the room. Jackie took charge at 1:00 p.m. sharp. She thanked Mr. Moore and Mr. White for their attendance. She introduced Nivea to everyone in the room. Nivea remained standing as Johnathan moved to her side and began to speak.

"Nivea and I put together the plans and cost estimates of a new building, which would be the first on site, privately owned state-of-the-art laboratory, on a multidiversified farm in the United States. It would have the capability to run any chemical and biological evaluations needed by any farming industry in the state or nation. It would also be able to test the purity, strength, and genetics of any animal or plant DNA, all of which would be critical in the Cannabis business for a multitude of reasons."

Nivea took over, "The projected building would be 50'×200' and constructed of cement blocks." Nivea then projected, from her laptop, cost projections for all to see: Total cost of approximately $1 million. The costs in each category have a 10 percent increase built in for inflation that would cover one year only. The construction phase was $450,000 and the laboratory equipment $550,000. "We feel the laboratory, on its own, could generate enough income to stand on its own financially without the testing involved with Cannabis but had a risk factor. We recommend a hold on any construction until we see how things unfold."

Jackie then stood. "Thank you, Johnathan and Nivea, for such a timely report. Medical use of cannabis is coming in the state of Pennsylvania and, I believe, recreational use legalized shortly thereafter. Much like with gambling, the politicians see a source of revenue they will not be able to resist. As we pursue this option as a possible means of sustaining this farm well into the future, we must position ourselves politically. The left of center Democrats will not be an issue. It will be the right of center Republicans that we will need to help achieve our business agenda on the state level."

Billy concluded, "Grandma and Papa, Mom and Dad, Jackie and I need your help to pull this off. We need you to get us connected in the Republican Party in Crawford County. We cannot do this without your connections. This vital assistance is required for this project to even get off the ground. Once Jackie and I get in and get established, we can handle the rest and get where we need to be at the state level to make good decisions for this farm. We need you to open the door."

Martha stood and said, "We have the key, and we will unlock the door." This was the first time in years Grandma and Papa had been called upon in a board meeting to help Eagle's Nest, and they relished in the idea that they were still needed.

Jackie looked at Billy and whispered, "Timing is everything. We will meet in two weeks." They formed the circle and held hands as Jackie spoke, "Dear God, bless my husband, our family, our friends, and bless this farm. Amen. Adjourned."

Mr. Moore and Mr. White looked at each other and could not believe what they had just witnessed. It seemed that everyone stayed longer than usual. Many questions were asked, and the conversations were centered around the business but also about the lives of the four interns. Congratulations were offered by all in attendance.

Billy said, "What a great job by all." The four were proud of their work. Billy asked, "Dad, can the four of us have the afternoon off?"

Will responded, "You sure deserve it. You have put in a ton of hours in the last two weeks. You have this afternoon and tomorrow off. Relax and enjoy each other's company. I want you to be back by 7:00 p.m. Your mother and I have invited your grandparents over for dinner and would like you to be here. Optional for Team Johnathan."

When Billy delivered the news, it was nice to feel appreciated, and they all needed the break to rest and to get caught up on their paperwork for their internships. Team Johnathan was leaving and heading to Erie for dinner and an overnight stay and a work/play session. They would be back early evening tomorrow. Jackie and Billy decided just to hang out in their room and spend some quiet time together.

Taking a shower was one of life's pleasures for Jackie. When done, she threw a robe onto her body and started her assigned responsibility to Mr. White. Billy was on the bed, in his boxers, educating himself on Colorado's and Washington's history related to legalizing Cannabis for medical and recreational use. After an hour of typing and completing her weekly assignment, Jackie walked over to the bed, opened her robe to her man, let it slide off her shoulders, and snuggled up next to her husband. They set their alarm for 5:30 p.m. and fell into a deep sleep in each other's arms. It was what they needed more than anything. Tomorrow, they would find time to fulfill their partner's needs.

They awoke and texted Milly they would pick up Grandma and Papa. They left at 6:00 p.m. so they could spend time with them alone before going back to the farm for dinner. They entered, and hugs were exchanged.

"Sounds like we get a chance to help. It's about time," said Grandma. "Papa and I will get you a schedule of all meetings and meet and greets scheduled by the Crawford County Republican Committee for the rest of this year. We will take you wherever and whenever you want to go and introduce you to all of our political friends. We can arrange meeting the state representatives and senators from the three-county area. I can squeeze real hard and get you a meeting with our congressmen and senators, if you're willing to travel. I can work both sides of the aisle to get you two in the political eye in Northwestern Pennsylvania and the state."

"Thanks, Grandma. Whatever you and Papa can do will really help."

It was apparent after dinner, they were going to have lots of help from both parents and grandparents. They would soon find out just how much political capital these two generations had earned over the last half-century. They both knew it was time to spend some of that capital and how important it was for Billy and Jackie to be able to make the right decision for the farm. They were all in. It became increasingly apparent how lively and energetic William and Martha had become with this new assignment put on them by their grandchildren.

On the way home, Jackie told her grandma and papa, "I need you to make a report on your progress at the next business meeting. That will be February 7." Jackie walked them in and said goodbye with a hug and kiss.

"I sure do love that girl."

"Me, too, William."

\* \* \* \* \*

The four interns returned to work on Friday and were totally refreshed and emotionally charged due to their extra rest and amorous activities. The time off was just what they needed. They met at 8:00 a.m. in the boardroom. It was evident that each team had already determined what needed done next. They were turning into a very productive group that would have to be reckoned with by their adversaries. Their meeting lasted all of ten minutes, and they broke up to get their work done. Team Johnathan made their daily morning visits to both the bovine and grain portions of the farm. The foreman and employees actually started looking forward to their daily chats with Team Johnathan. They were back at the boardroom working on the project by 10:45 a.m.

Jackie was up early as usual. It was beginning to be a habit of hers to go to the window and enjoy the view that the window offered. Since the morning of her wedding, she was seeing the eagles every morning. She kept this to herself and pondered its significance. Her instincts, for the first time, were foggy and unclear.

The four interns decided that they would dress formally for today's meeting. It was nice getting out of their daily casual work clothes and dress up for the meeting. They were at the table at 6:30 a.m. as required by the terms of their internship. Will and Milly were already seated, enjoying their coffee.

Milly looked surprised when she saw them entering the kitchen. "You four look awesome. What's the occasion?"

"We all decided to dress up for the meeting today," said Nivea.

"Well, you all look very professional," replied Will.

A collective *thanks* was heard simultaneously.

"Are you and Dad ready for today?"

"We sure are," said Milly. "We decided to let Grandma Martha and Papa do their presentation to make them feel even more involved. Will and I will run the projection from the laptop." All four interns smiled and could not wait for the meeting and the presentation from this very respected couple.

The February 7, 2019, meeting started at 1:00 p.m. sharp.

Johnathan and Nivea stood up, and Johnathan spoke first, "Nivea and I have met with the foreman and employees every morning before 9:00 a.m. since we started our work here. I am glad to report that we have not lost any cows since they were interned for the winter in the barn. We currently have enough food on site to carry them till May, if necessary. These daily meeting have generated some ideas which could possibly improve the efficiency on both sides of the business."

Nivea enthusiastically began, "I have started running chemical analysis on our fuel that is being fed into our methane-generating system to help evaluate which fuels generate more methane and why. Johnathan and I are also studying biomass production per plant with Cannabis. If and when we get started, we need to know how to maximize the production of each plant to improve profit margins. Finally, we are currently involved in identifying Cannabis strains based on the chemical composition of the leaves, buds, and seeds. This will be essential to identify the strains based on their potency and growth rates. It will also allow us to verify the plants that are purchased are authentic. We can also invest in laboratory equipment that will allow us to determine DNA tags to identify these strains quickly and more accurately."

Jackie began, "Team Johnathan, thank you again for your informative and enlightening report. You two work well together and do amazing work for this farm." Will was again impressed with his interns!

"Billy and I have been looking into the political issues that arose prior to legalizing medical, and then recreational, marijuana, the restrictions placed on the growth and sale of the product, the taxes and licensing fees for growers and sellers of the product. We also have looked into how those states have used the revenues generated. There are so many variables in this equation.

"One thing we know for sure from the business end of this proposition is we would need to be the only producer in the state, or one of two at the most. We would require a contract from the state that would guarantee a period of time to be licensed so we can recoup our investment and be compensated sufficiently to make the process worthwhile. A contract must give us the ability to grow, test, package, and distribute the product for reasons that will be explained at a later time if and when needed. Now I would like to turn the meeting over to William and Martha McDonald."

They were also dressed professionally. William stood as Will and Milly manned the laptop. William started, "Copies of the material presented on the screen are at the head of the table and available for your use at the end of the meeting. The first screen shows every legislative district in the state with the representative's name, office address, office phone number, email, and party affiliation. Next, please. The same information appears except it is for state senators. Next, please. The next ten screens contain the voting records of every state representative and state senator on anything closely related to marijuana in the last two years, their current stand on legalizing marijuana for medical purposes and for recreational use, and any public statements related to either. Next, please. A complete list of every member of both the Crawford County Republican and Democratic Committees with the same personal information that was listed for the Pennsylvania state representatives and senators."

"Next, please," Martha continued as William sat. "Finally, I have arranged the following scheduled meetings that must be attended by both Billy and Jackie." On the screen appeared a list of meetings with dates, times, and locations, with a wide variety of local committee people, state representative, state senators, a liaison to the governor, two US congressmen, and the two US senators from Pennsylvania.

The first generation of McDonalds just spent a large piece of political capital they had earned over the last fifty years of their lives. Every scheduled meeting was within one calendar month of today's meeting. Everyone in the room looked in awe at what they just witnessed.

Billy and Jackie stood first, followed by Will, Milly, Mr. Moore, Mr. White, Johnathan, and Nivea, and all clapped in unison for the great presentation by the most senior McDonalds.

Jackie looked and whispered to Billy, "Timing is everything." A circle was formed. "God bless my husband, this family, our friends, and this farm. Amen. Adjourned." Again, everyone stayed and talked.

It was apparent these young people in charge of Eagle's Nest had a unique way of making everybody feel part of the team and part of the success. Will and Milly took Will's parents home after the meeting and got them inside their house. "Son, you know we have been truly blessed by the arrival of these young people at the farm."

"Yes, I know. Milly and I have been truly blessed to have you and Mom still in our lives. We love you."

"Your mother and I love you too."

# Chapter 13

The Fab 4 returned to the farmhouse looking for food and clothes. They raided the fridge and found lunch meat and apple pie. They cleaned up, set the table for two, and headed upstairs to change their clothes. Before they climbed the stairs to their rooms, they stopped to talk in the living room.

Billy asked, "Do you know specifically what's next for you two?"

"Not sure, Billy," replied Johnathan

"Why don't you guys take the next month and lay out your 50×200 building in greater detail. Try to determine the exact equipment and square footage needed to test the potency of the weed if we start growing. Determine the equipment and space needed to do the DNA testing. Finally, see if you can come up with a secure method of logging and tracking our packaged goods as they move from here to arrival at the dispensaries. I'm sure the state will want to track this shit from the time we get the plants till the time it is bought and delivered to the dispensaries. We need to have our system in place and ready to go if we want to have a chance. I also want to make sure we have the space and equipment to run all other biological and chemical testing to help our farming community friends."

"Sounds like a lot of work, but we will get done what we can in the month we have been given," replied Johnathan.

"Please determine if our laboratory is big enough for all our needs and if our equipment budget is adequate. We may not see you guys that much in the next month. It looks like Grandma and Papa have our show on the road for the next month. Johnathan and Nivea, there may be times when we will need both of you to help us out at parties or social gathering with politicians in attendance. It is always nice to have smart young couples with beautiful women to grab the attention of a male politician or vice versa. Whenever possible, we will give you as much notice as we can."

They both smiled and were on their way to change. Billy and Jackie did the same.

"Billy, I was always a beautiful girl, and I am now a beautiful woman. I have been pursued for years by men that were not worthy of me, until I met you. Then I pursued you. I will be by your side this next month, looking as beautiful as I can possibly be. I will dress tastefully, be extremely intelligent, and be at your side at all times. I promise when we get home at night, I will be yours until morning. I love you, William 'Billy' McDonald III."

Jackie began taking off her clothes and did what she always did when she wanted to relax, and that was shower. Billy followed, and they entered the shower together. Within minutes, the groans and moans of love resonated from the shower and lasted for at least a half hour. They returned to the bedroom completely dried by the other and began to dress for the late afternoon and evening. Jackie put on her panties and jeans. Billy was surprised but not disappointed when she chose a white blouse and no bra. There was not much left to his imagination as her perfectly shaped breasts and nipples projected through her white blouse. Billy knew he would be ambushed by his wife tonight! He looked forward with anticipation!

Billy and Jackie were working their way through their appointments and meetings with great success. They were an impressive couple. She was beautiful, charming, and intelligent. He was handsome, virile, and also intelligent. Grandma and Papa had scheduled their meetings to work from the bottom up on the political food chain. They were very wise in the sequencing of their appointments. They moved from the county to the state level, and people in both parties were starting to talk about them both as great potential candidates for state offices but also a potential congressional bid, even though neither had ever run for office. The third week in February contained only two meetings: one as guest of the local congressman to attend a congressional party with a short list of guests, and the other a twenty-minute sit-down with one of Pennsylvania's senators. It really did not matter which one to the McDonalds, as they were quickly learning how the game was played.

The congressional black-tie event was well attended. Rumors were spreading Jackie would be running for Congress next term, and they had to get a look. Jackie was in a full-length flowing black evening gown with spaghetti straps and a slit to midthigh. Her bosoms were pushed up and exposed with style and grace. Her black hair was wavy and below her shoulders. Her dark eyes against her dark hair accentuated the look in her eyes, which could penetrate your soul in a millisecond. She wore a pair of elegant diamond earrings that hung softly from her ears and were complemented by an elegant diamond necklace.

Billy leaned over and said to Jackie, "Let's dance and circle the dance floor twice so these politicians won't hurt their necks stretching to see your beauty."

She smiled and grabbed Billy's hand gracefully as they moved to the dance floor. They mingled and talked with most everyone in attendance as the evening waned. They had accomplished what they had set out to do, and no one present had a clue what it was. They were one of the last to leave, and when they did, they thanked their congressman for their invitation and handed him a check for ten thousand dollars.

They were up early, showered, ate breakfast, and were off to their ten o'clock with the senator from Pennsylvania. Jackie and Billy discussed the possibility he already knew of his wife's beauty and their $10,000 donation to their congressman. Jackie, again, looked seductively beautiful, only this time, in less-formal clothing.

Billy was not surprised at the senator's directness when he asked, "Do either of you have intentions of running for any state or federal office?"

Jackie responded with a beautiful smile and a look which penetrated the senator's very being, "We are undecided." Ten minutes later, they left the senator's office and assured each other that mission

DC was a complete and a total success. In a very short time, they had become skilled players in the game of politics.

The rest of the day was spent touring DC. It was a beautiful day with no wind, the sun was shining, and the sky was clear; it was truly a beautiful day for a stroll about in the nation's capital. They clasped each other's hand, and they were off. Most of their touring was external viewing as they walked about the capital. They took many pictures and asked a fellow tourist if she would mind taking a picture of them in front of the Lincoln Memorial.

They were most impressed with the quiet solitude and solemnness that was heavy in the air as they walked the Vietnam Memorial.

Jackie said to Billy, "I am absolutely amazed at the sheer number of names on this wall. These men and women made the ultimate sacrifice for a country that had the least respect for them and their comrades of any generation of soldier in American history." No other words were spoken as they stood and viewed the Wall. It was heartbreaking to see row after row after row of names of young men and women inscribed in the black cold stone who had made the ultimate sacrifice in the jungles, hills, and rice paddies of Vietnam.

Their flight from DC to Pittsburgh to Erie was scheduled for ten o'clock in the morning, so they decided to have an early dinner in their hotel. They called ahead for reservations and got a table in an hour, just the time needed to walk back to the hotel. Their table was ready for them when they arrived, and they both relaxed, enjoyed their food, wine, and the other's company. Two and a half hours later, they returned to their room. They showered together as usual, and when they got into bed, they quickly fell into a deep sleep in each other's arms.

## Chapter 14

Johnathan and Nivea picked them up at the Erie International Airport as scheduled.

Johnathan asked, "How was Washington, DC? How was the party? How did the senator treat you?"

"Slow down, Johnathan. One at a time."

Billy and Jackie shared their whole story with their friends as they returned to the farm.

They were, again, hit with another onslaught of questions as soon as they entered the back door and entered the kitchen. As hungry as Jackie was for food, the rest of the McDonald clan were hungrier for information.

"I'm hungry. Let's fix some breakfast." Everyone jumped to Jackie's request and, together, began making breakfast as Billy and Jackie explained their last three days in Washington, DC, amid the flurry of activity. By the time they had finished eating and finished their coffee, they had answered all their questions and explained why their trip was so successful. After listening to their report, the two generations of older McDonalds realized that their beautiful daughter was a tiger to be reckoned with, and one would be wise to stay out of her way. When it came to her beloved Billy, her new family, or Eagle's Nest, there would be no retreat. Jackie thanked everyone for helping them in their part of this massive project.

"Johnathan, how have you guys been making out on your end?"

"We are progressing faster than we thought originally. There is a ton of work in that request you gave to Nivea and me."

"I know. Is there any way we can have a report to date if we call a meeting for this coming Wednesday?"

"Sure, we can do that." As Johnathan looked at Nivea, she nodded in agreement.

"I will let Moore and White know today. Johnathan and Nivea, Billy and I would like you both to attend the annual Crawford County Republican dinner and fundraiser with us next Thursday evening. If you can go, that will make eight. Please check your schedules, and let us know. I would like to overwhelm them by the attendance of the four most beautiful women in Crawford County."

"Dad, can your Fab 4 have a four-day weekend on March 1, 2, 3, and 4? Billy and I would like to treat Johnathan and Nivea to a two-night, all-expenses-paid stay at Niagara Falls. We want them to know how much we appreciate them as friends and for all of their hard work they have put into the success of this farm and this family."

"I think that it is a great idea. So be it." All four smiled at the older McDonalds, and each thanked them.

"Your father and I will give both Johnathan and Nivea five hundred dollars each to spend as they wish on this well-deserved break." Johnathan and Nivea could not have been more appreciative.

Nivea replied, "I love being here with you. I love my work here. I love working on different projects, I love being appreciated, I love you Johnathan, and I love this family."

When they left the table and the impromptu meeting, Nivea asked Johnathan, "Why had Billy and Jackie not been offered the five hundred dollars?"

"I guess the McDonalds expect more of family than guests." It was not a lie, and it satisfied Nivea's curiosity. Johnathan knew that the trait had been passed to Billy and accepted by Jackie. They would not be outworked!

When Billy and Jackie arrived at the boardroom, they found Team Johnathan at work looking over a copy of the drawings for the proposed new building. They had made many adjustments to the original, as the needs were changing. They both had several pages of notes written on their legal pads.

"Where are you guys at this point with the building?"

"We should be able to keep it the same size as originally planned. We will have enough room and equipment to test anything we need to test. It will be no problem testing the amount of weed required to supply all the estimated twenty-five dispensaries. We will also have room to be able to run DNA testing to verify what plants we are really dealing with. As you know, each different strain has different potencies. We will have an area about 50×50 leftover for the biology and chemical analysis portion of the lab. This 50×200 building will have to be built in such a way to expand when necessary. We are working on that now. Functional, same size, and same cost to get started, assuming medical marijuana comes first and followed by recreational use a year or two later. We will need to keep our proverbial noses up the politician's asses between now and then."

The meeting scheduled for Wednesday, February 28, 2019, began at 1:00 p.m. sharp.

Team Billy decided that Billy would explain their last month's activities.

"Thanks, Grandma and Papa for laying out a great month of appointments for Jackie and me. Your progression of meetings was perfect for accomplishing our goals. Our goal was to make contact with the people in power at the local, state, and federal levels of the Republican and Democratic Parties. Mission accomplished. Our goal was to let them see the great potential we both had as possible candidates for public office. Mission accomplished. Our goal was to expose them to Jackie. They needed to see her intelligence, her ability to persuade, her stunning beauty, and her cunning up close and personal. Mission accomplished. Rumor has it that you are in the presence of the next congresswoman or senator from the great state of Pennsylvania." Billy laughed and clapped his hands, and Jackie stood up and took a bow.

"Our goal was to let them know we had money to spend. Mission accomplished."

Grandma said, "You must have done well. My phone has been lighting up for days. Political friends and acquaintances we have not heard from in years wanting to know where you were going to be next."

Jackie stated, "This is all thanks to you and Papa. In the very near future, we will need a platform to speak, and people will have to take us seriously or fear opposition from the McDonald clan. Billy and I will continue to make our rounds, make calls, send emails, and attend functions. Only now, we will start pushing the agenda for legalizing medical marijuana in the state of Pennsylvania. Team Johnathan has been working diligently but have nothing to report at this time. A reminder to the McDonald family and Team Johnathan, we'll be attending the Crawford County Republican dinner and fundraiser tomorrow evening."

The dinner was a who's who of Crawford County Republicans. The conversations seemed to dwindle when the eight gusts from the Eagle's Nest walked in. Within minutes, people began to make their way slowly but surely toward the McDonald clan to shake hands, welcome them, and to admire the pure beauty of the girl they had heard so much about through the rumor mills. Jackie did not disappoint.

The dinner and dance was a tradition in Crawford County politics for the Republicans. There was nothing traditional about the excitement that was generated by the young couple they all had heard so much about. They could not believe how easy they could converse with everyone they met, their intelligence on a wide variety of topics, their composure, their good looks, and the energy they generated by their presence in the room. Johnathan and Nivea were at their side all night and were equally impressive. Team Billy and Team Johnathan stole the show.

The four-day break was a welcomed relief for the Fab 4. They enjoyed dancing, dining, gambling, sightseeing, and each other's company for four days. They were completely rejuvenated mentally, physically, and emotionally. Tuesday morning's six thirty breakfast found the Fab 4 in playful, energetic conversation as they relived the highlights of the previous four days. Work assignments were being discussed as they walked out the back door into the cool crisp air of the early morning.

## Chapter 15

The month of March just flew by, and the meeting scheduled for Wednesday, April 3, 2019, began at 1:00 p.m. sharp.

Nivea rose first and began, "In front of every chair are the approved architectural drawings for the new laboratory. Additional papers included the final layout of the laboratory, stations, and equipment placement within the laboratory. A complete laboratory equipment inventory listing, equipment and consumables, and the cost of all items. Finally, we have put together a comparison of hydroponics versus soil growth, the benefits of each, and cost comparisons between the two."

Jackie stood. "The papers you have in front of you represent hours and hours of work by both Johnathan and Nivea. They have worked very hard and have done a professional job throughout this whole process. Everyone in the McDonald family thanks you for your efforts, and we all love you guys. Billy and I will be making a final decision on this project within the week. We would appreciate your opinion as to the soundness of this business venture for the future of Eagle's Nest. We need you all to digest everything presented today and make an honest report to Billy and me by this time Friday, April 5, 2019."

Billy stood and began, "These are the facts and our predictions based on information we have collected to this point in time. We will be honest. This is our best-guess scenario. The state of Pennsylvania will pass a bill that will legalize medical marijuana in the next two years. Seventy-five percent of all state representatives and senators have indicated that they would vote for such a bill. The numbers are fifty-fifty when it comes to legalizing marijuana for recreational use."

"Billy, what do you see as the expected revenues and expenditures if you decide to proceed with this project?" asked Mr. Moore.

"Records indicate states that already have legalized medical marijuana with populations smaller than Pennsylvania have recorded minimum total sales of over $100 million per year. The state will make sure it gets its 30 percent in tax revenue from the sale of the weed at the dispensaries. They will also receive revenue from licensing and fees from the grower to the dispensaries. The dispensaries will get their cut also. I estimate about $45 million left for the grower and labs. Expenditures will consume 85 percent to 90 percent of that total, leaving approximately 10 percent or $4.5 million in profit for one year. That would be equal to $31.5 million in projected revenues over the life of the contract. We have estimated income low and our costs high to ensure the feasibility of our financial statements in our projections. We will only consider this project if we get a minimum seven-year contract to produce, analyze, and verify—quality assurance—of the weed for all the dispensaries throughout the state."

Jackie added, "Johnathan and Nivea have already devised a method of biologically tagging the plants, whether grown by soil or by hydroponics, to satisfy any requirement the state may place on following the product from the growing site to the lab and on to the sale at the dispensary. We are still working out a process to package and ship the product."

"Jackie could you explain your considerations relative to growing hydroponic or by soil?

"Papa, I think I will let Johnathan explain. This is more in his area of expertise."

"Hydroponics is a much more expensive way to grow any crop. It is most often done indoors, and that in itself requires a tremendous expenditure for the building and the lighting necessary to grow a large biomass of product. The biomass produced from hydroponics also tends to be smaller than product grown in sunlight. Plants require light to grow, and there is no substitute for the amount of light the sun produces.

"The positives are that you can more directly control what goes into the plant by what is added to its water environment. The other item is the building in which your product is grown, by its nature, creates greater security for the product being grown. In our case, one marijuana plant is worth much more than a stalk of corn, if you get my drift. Finally, you can control the environment much better. Your crop will never experience a drought or a frost and can be grown in the winter months if desired. Does that answer your question, William?"

"Thanks, Johnathan."

Jackie thanked Johnathan and continued, "It is our intention to proceed with building and the supplying of our laboratory. It will financially support itself running a wide variety of biological and chemical tests for the agricultural industry in the tristate area and diversify the farm even more. We will continue to pursue all avenues that would allow us to be in a position of strength relative to the state legalizing medical marijuana if and when it makes its move. We will continue to aggressively pursue all aspects of this project as if it were to start tomorrow. Please let us know any suggestions, questions, concerns, or opinions that you have on these matters by Friday."

Jackie looked at Billy and whispered, "Timing is everything." Hands were held in a circle as Jackie said, "Bless my husband, this family, our friends, and this farm. Amen. Adjourned."

## Chapter 16

The feedback was positive by all who attended Wednesday's meeting. Everyone was impressed with the idea of the laboratory being built as soon as possible. They were impressed with the work that had been done so far. All were impressed with the additional diversity added to the farm's portfolio with the addition of the lab. Most of all, they seemed to be impressed with the business maturity that these young folks exhibited in their decision-making process.

The time was 6:30 p.m., and the meeting after the meeting had yet to adjourn. They knew there were serious issues that still needed their immediate attention. Security of their crop and farm, percent of their operation that should or could be hydroponics, the cost of heat and utilities to the hydroponic buildings, process to evaluate the progression of a potential bill in the state house and senate.

They returned to the farmhouse at the bidding of Milly after just starting a discussion on the best placement of their laboratory relative to the future building sites. It was 7:30 p.m.

Milly and Will fed the Fab 4 and told them, "We will clean up after you eat."

Johnathan and Nivea put on a light coat and sat on the porch swing, and Billy and Jackie went on a walkabout.

\* \* \* \* \*

A well-hidden tape recorder had been turned on prior to their entrance as Jackie and Billy welcomed their state representative and senator for their districts into their boardroom.

Jackie had taken some extra time getting herself ready for this meeting. She had brushed her hair, light amount of eyeshadow, and light color of lipstick, tight jeans, and white blouse unbuttoned enough to excite but not expose unless a forward lean. They had met several times before, and their representatives heard and believed the rumors of their guest's political prowess. They would not be disappointed.

Jackie and Billy welcomed them warmly and made them feel comfortable in the lavish boardroom of the Eagle's Nest. This was not what the representatives expected. Johnathan and Nivea then entered and were introduced. That was the end of the pleasantries as Jackie took over the room and the conversation. When she was done, they knew exactly what was requested of them.

They were told, "Your vote is not necessary for medical marijuana legislation to pass. It is going to pass in the next two years. Eagle's Nest is actively going to politically pursue a seven-year contract with the state of Pennsylvania for the sole right to grow, analyze, tag, and ship medical marijuana to all the dispensaries in the state. It would result in an influx of $34 million into their district and a landfall of $30 to $40 million into the state treasury every year, hundreds of jobs, and you would be heroes in the end. We are not asking for your vote. We are asking that you use every political chip you have to make sure it happens."

They unveiled the drawings of their state-of-the-art laboratory that would be built within the year at a cost of $1 million. If they wanted to become part of their team, they would be welcomed and kept up to date as things progressed. If not, they might find a very well-funded primary challenger come next election.

"What do you think?"

"Did you just threaten us, Mrs. McDonald?"

"Heavens no. We just gave you some options. All are positive for you and your careers. Vote against the medical marijuana bill, and you keep your Republican constituents happy. Do everything in your power to create hundreds of jobs with a corresponding influx of several millions of dollars into the district, and you keep your Republican constituents happy. This is going to happen in some district. It might as well be yours. Again, you keep your constituents happy. I am just making you aware of a possible scenario in which you and your constituents win twice, and we win once. That does not sound like a threat to me, gentlemen, just sound political advice."

Jackie leaned forward to look directly into their eyes.

"I see what you mean, Mrs. McDonald," said the senator.

"Please, call me Jackie!" She stood erect. They all smiled, shook hands, and the Fab 4 escorted their representatives to their cars.

They returned to the boardroom, and Billy, Johnathan, and Nivea could not believe Jackie had just told them what they were going to do, why they were going to do it, why both parties would benefit, and sent them on their way. They all agreed she would make a great trial lawyer.

Billy asked Johnathan, who, now, had been entrusted with the combination to the safe, "Please put the tape recording away."

It was not coincidence that Will and Milly were not home that day. Jackie wanted them as far away from the farm as possible when those two guests were to arrive. If they were not home, they could not say that either of the representatives had been there that day. All on tape, neat and clean. Jackie left nothing to chance. She was as cunning as she was beautiful.

The Fab 4 decided to cook steaks on the grill and eat at the formal dining room table that night. Steak, baked potatoes, green beans, salad, wine, bread, and conversation was the menu for the evening. They enjoyed a wonderful evening with their best friends talking, laughing, drinking, and reminiscing.

At some point, Nivea said, "Oh my god! We have less than three weeks left in our internship."

Johnathan and Nivea, all of a sudden, developed this blank stare on their face, and the conversation ceased but only temporarily. Conversation diminished around eleven. They cleaned up, put everything in its place—it was ready for breakfast—and headed upstairs for the evening.

When Jackie and Billy entered their room, Jackie immediately said to Billy, "What are we going to do when our friends leave when their internship is done?"

"We make them an offer they can't refuse. Did you forget? We are millionaires!"

Jackie removed her clothes, put on her robe, and headed for the shower. She was surprised when Billy didn't come in to join her. She had hoped he would. She needed and wanted her man. Jackie simply put the robe on her shoulders and walked toward the bed. When she was almost there, she lost the robe, and immediately, the blankets rose where Billy's manhood was located. Apparently, Billy needed and wanted his woman too. By morning, they had more than satisfied the other's needs.

Around the breakfast table, everyone looked relaxed and at peace with themselves.

Apparently, Team Johnathan had also met each other's needs during the evening. Both couples did not make it to the table until 10:00 a.m.

Johnathan told Billy, "We would like to take you and Jackie out for breakfast this morning."

Billy said, "Let's go. I will drive. Where are we going, you two?"

Nivea answered excitedly as they all jumped into the car, "Take us to Perkins in Meadville."

Johnathan and Nivea were uncharacteristically quiet in the car and during breakfast. After they finished breakfast—

"Jackie and Billy, Nivea and I got engaged this morning in the shower."

"That is awesome. Some really great things happen in the shower," Jackie said with a big smile.

Nivea then moved her left hand toward them, showing off her beautiful ring to her two best friends. "Oh, honey, it's beautiful."

Upon returning, they entered the house to find Will and Milly home. "Mr. and Mrs. McDonald, look at my beautiful ring! Johnathan and I got engaged last night." Nivea was anxious to show her ring to their adopted parents.

"We could not be happier for you two kids. You both are wonderful people whom we have grown to love and appreciate more and more every day."

Johnathan spoke up, "Thank you, you two. You have been good to both of us. We appreciate everything. We have tried to please you as if you were our own parents during this internship and stay in your home."

Will assured them, "We have been very pleased with your work, your character, and your love and friendship toward this family."

Team Johnathan excused themselves.

"What if Jackie and I want to hire Team Johnathan when their internship is over? How would we go about paying their salaries and their benefits? Would it come out of the farm's general fund, or would they be paid from the account with the $3 million we inherited?"

"Good question, Billy. I think it would come out of the general fund, since all other employees are paid from that fund. We need to ask Mr. Moore to be sure."

Billy thought for a moment and then spoke, "Either way, we need them. We cannot proceed without them. I am going to offer them a team contract for one year at $190,000 and full benefits. They are worth twice that to Jackie and me."

"I agree they are essential until we get this decided. If this works out, you will need them for the rest of their careers."

Jackie and Billy headed to the boardroom to try and hire their best friends. They took a bottle of wine and four wine glasses.

Johnathan asked, "What is the deal with the wine and glasses?"

Jackie told them, "We are going to celebrate your engagement and your new job on the same day."

Nivea, again, asked, "What are you two talking about?"

"You two got engaged today, did you not?"

"Yes."

"You also got hired today. Billy and I just hired Team Johnathan on a one-year contract at $190,000, plus full benefits. What do you guys think?"

They looked at Billy and Jackie and said collectively, "Open the bottle."

## Chapter 17

"Jackie and Billy sure have alleviated any stress we may have encountered trying to find jobs that would be close together. We are engaged, love one another, have jobs that we love, and love our employer. We might as well set a date. What do you think, Johnathan?"

So went the morning conversation in the shower in Team Johnathan's room. Down the hall, in Team Billy's room, Jackie was standing in front of the window admiring the view as Billy slept. The eagles were soaring again. They had become more and more frequent visitors to the skies of Eagle's Nest. Jackie loved to watch them in the morning and felt some kindred spirt between the three of them, but her instincts still told her nothing about the significance of their return and their majestic flight. It bothered her.

Jackie's phone rang. It was a conference call with their local legislative representatives. They sounded enthusiastic and extremely positive in the process of trying to set a meeting for the afternoon with Jackie.

"We are having a team meeting but will see you around two if you can make it then."

"Perfect, we will see you then."

When the legislators entered the boardroom, they were surprised to see the table completely covered with architectural drawings of the new building. Present were three generations of McDonalds and Team Johnathan, busily talking while they looked at the drawings. Nivea had turned on the recorder as soon as they entered the long driveway heading toward the boardroom.

Jackie spoke first, "Welcome to the Eagle's Nest, gentlemen. I believe you know everyone here. Can I get you anything to drink before we begin?"

"No thanks."

"What can we do for you today?"

Jackie was being aggressive and not giving an inch with her opening volley.

"We both met and considered your suggestions and have both agreed to move forward in an attempt to acquire support for your business proposal that would benefit the citizens of Northwestern Pennsylvania."

"To what specific proposal are you referring? We discussed several when we met the other day."

"The proposal to support your effort to acquire the contract that would allow you to grow, test, tag, and ship all marijuana to the medical marijuana dispensaries throughout the Commonwealth."

Martha spoke, "John and Dennis, I think you two have made a wise choice. You certainly have convinced this group of constituents that you deserve our support. We will support you in any way possible if you follow through on your promises to improve the economics of this area. FYI, Jackie and Billy are now the ultimate decision-makers for this family and this farm. They will contact you. Please do not take them lightly. They are a couple to be reckoned with. Thank you both for coming to see us today. We all appreciate your time."

Grandma had again surprised everyone. It could not have been more perfectly played. Jackie set them up, and they took the bait and vocalized their part in this effort on tape. Grandma let them know that the McDonald clan expected a follow-through on their part or no support would be given toward their reelection efforts.

They understood completely the spoken and the unspoken language in their meeting with the McDonalds. They said their goodbyes and headed toward their car. Billy and Jackie thanked everyone for working on the building project and for their perfect teamwork in the presence of the politicians. On that note, anyone over twenty-five departed the room.

Team Johnathan added a few last items to the change list to be given to the architect.

Team Billy excused themselves to go to Billy's office across the hall to rattle a few chains. Billy started composing a letter that would follow Jackie's phone calls and their second visit to Washington, DC. The emails would be sent to all eighteen US congressmen's private servers at their Washington offices.

All eighteen had been at the dinner dance and had been exposed to the beauty of Jackie and the rumors of her political power and money. Sixteen of the eighteen gathered for the meeting and luncheon put on by the McDonalds. Some congressmen were there out of curiosity, to see for themselves how this woman handled herself in a meeting. Some were there just to get a closer glimpse of this intriguing women. A few of the congressmen were there because they felt it was just a good move and politically expedient. No expense was spared, and the congressmen were impressed. They were about to be impressed even more.

Lunch was over when Jackie took the microphone and started to walk among the tables, explaining their business plan to their state's congressmen. All eyes were on Jackie as she moved about the room. It was definitely a captive audience! Jackie, as always, looked beautiful, spoke intelligently, and had them mesmerized.

Jackie stressed that having a centrally located site would save the state hundreds of thousands in bureaucratic costs. There would be less chance of illegal activities if all product were produced, processed, tested, and shipped from a single site. The single site could be checked more frequently to ensure the whole process, from growth, tagging, packaging, and shipping, was being operated to state standards. Jackie exposed them to the projection of revenues based on other states that legalized marijuana for medicinal use. Pennsylvania's cut, based on a taxing rate of 35 percent and revenues generated from licensing fees from producer to testing labs to dispensaries, would be in the neighborhood of $40 million.

She proposed that the product was going to be produced, tested, tagged, and shipped somewhere in Pennsylvania, why not Northwestern Pennsylvania? She would appreciate their support in their home districts by talking to their local state representatives and senators about the Northwestern Pennsylvania option. She ensured them that they had already started a statewide political push for their Northwestern Pennsylvania option, and their local state representatives had already been contacted several times.

"I want to thank you for your attendance and support and look forward to working with you in the future. It is important that this remains a state issue and not a federal issue. If you would like to stick around and ask questions, please feel free. We will have an open bar for the next hour for your convenience."

Jackie and Billy were surprised when most of the congressmen stayed for a drink or two and asked important and significant questions. Most were, again, impressed with the couple and thought they would be the right choice to oversee this very important responsibility and assured them they would take the time to talk to local Pennsylvania representatives and senators or call them as soon as possible. Jackie and Billy cornered their own representative and let him know how much the McDonald family was looking forward to his support to enhance the economic development in his district. He was a smart man and understood what was not spoken.

Billy and Jackie avoided any alcohol during their get-together with the Pennsylvania congressmen. They were planning on driving home after the meeting. It was 4:00 p.m., and the I-495 and I-95 were packed with rush hour traffic. They decided to stay if they could get a room. Billy was able to get a room with a single call to the Madison. They were smart enough to think ahead and brought what they would need if they decided to stay.

"Johnathan, this is Billy. We will not be home till around 7:00 p.m. tomorrow evening. Would you please send the email that is on my computer in Dad's office, tomorrow morning at 7:00 a.m.? All you need to do is bring it up and hit send."

"How was your meeting with the congressmen?"

"It was fine. Jackie did a great job presenting our plan. You just never know the loyalties these people have in their history. Johnathan, we will see you tomorrow, and we can talk more. See you then. Remind me when we get home to talk to you about when we can start construction."

"See you tomorrow, Billy."

Jackie and Billy ate when they arrived at the Madison and retired early. It had been a very long day. They were up at 6:30 a.m. and enjoying DC in their early morning walkabout. They held each other's hand, talked about a wide variety of issues, enjoyed each other's company, and enjoyed the sights and sounds of the nation's capital as it woke up for another day of business. The conversation continued into their hotel room when they returned from their walk. It was then that Jackie, for the first time, told Billy about her early morning visits to their bedroom window and that she had been seeing this wondrous pair of eagles almost every morning. They showered, had breakfast, and began their return trip to Northwestern Pennsylvania.

# Chapter 18

The meeting scheduled for Wednesday, May 15, 2019, began at 1:00 p.m. sharp.

All were present and accounted for, with the addition of the contractor and the architect. Jackie rose and asked the two guests, "Have we met all our obligation to the controlling government agencies in relationship to this building project?" Both guests signified that the project could legally begin.

The representative from Associated Contractors said, "We can begin tomorrow."

"Make it so. Begin this project tomorrow. Any questions and/or problems will be addressed to either Johnathan or Nivea, who have overseen this project from the beginning. One or the other or both will be at the building site ever morning at 7:30 a.m. to check daily progress and answer any questions of either the contractor or the building inspector. You have their cell numbers. Do either of you gentlemen have any further comments? Thank you for your time today." The two men, taking their cue, got up from their seats and exited the boardroom.

Jackie recognized Nivea, "Although this is a large building, it is a simple building to construct in that it is a rectangle and made of block. Once the footer is in place, the block layers can come in and get the walls up. That would be followed by placement of metal roof trusses and attachment of the metal roof. From that point on, it slows down. If the weather is decent, then all should be accomplished in sixty working days. This is when the plumbers and electricians would begin laying pipe and conduit in and on the ground, with leads extending above the level of the concrete.

"The concrete will be poured, followed by the return of the plumbers, electricians, and heating and air-conditioning specialists. They all can now finish their work on the inside. This will take the most time because of the nature of feeding the lab areas with water, electricity, and gas. The lab stations, counters, and sinks will all need electric, gas, and water leads to them. To make a long story longer, we should be in this building by the end of the 2019 year if all goes as planned."

Johnathan stood. "The four of us have already started working on a marketing plan that will emphasize the chemical testing we can do on soil, air, and water. We will also be able to identify various types of insects, molds, and bacteria in and on plants, soil, and water. This lab will make recommendations to the farmer as to how to fix their problems working with the agricultural extension agencies within their county. We will have the capability to provide genetic and DNA testing of any living organism to our clients. If this laboratory does what we think it will do, it could net Eagle's Nest $300,000 in net income by the end of year 1 and $500,000 by the end of year 2. This is a win-win for this farm and its existence into the future, regardless of what happens with the marijuana situation."

Jackie spoke again, "Billy and I have been thinking and talking in our walkabouts that we may be wise to forego the growing aspect of cannabis and focus on getting a contract for the testing of the product only. The outlay of a large amount of capital is not justifiable and is risky in an ever-changing political environment. We also have decided we would not be comfortable with the security measures necessary to protect the crop, this farm, and the good people who live and work here from the bad guys."

"Jackie, may I speak freely?"

"Sure, you are a trusted member of this team."

"When this merger took place, I was skeptical of such young people stepping into a position of power to run this great farm. Mr. White and I have continually been amazed at the amount of work, thought, tenacity, and effort the four of you have put into this farm.

We have also been impressed with the teamwork that has developed within this family. The four of you are wise beyond your years. The statement you just made shows wisdom and good financial decision-making and planning. Mr. White and I are proud to work for you."

Jackie looked at Billy and whispered, "Timing is everything." They held hands and formed a circle. "God bless my husband, this family, our friends, and this farm. Amen. Adjourned."

Mr. White and Mr. Moore were the first to leave. The older McDonalds approached the Fab 4 and gave each of them a hug and a quiet thank you as they left the boardroom. The Fab 4 smiled at one another as they realized how much they were respected, appreciated, and loved. It was a good feeling.

It was 7:00 a.m., Thursday, May 16, 2019, and the roar of diesel engines could be heard approaching Eagle's Nest. A convoy of tractors and trailers with their loads of heavy equipment pulled up the paved driveway. Jackie, Billy, Johnathan, Nivea, William, and Milly were there to meet them. The digging equipment was quickly removed from the lowboy trailers, and the trucks and their trailers were gone as quickly as they appeared. The equipment was moved to a site about one hundred yards from the grain elevators. The dozers had the ground leveled to the specifications of the laser transits by noon.

A perfect rectangle was laid out and the corners squared by one o'clock. The crews returned to their equipment at two, and the three backhoes started digging their 3-foot-wide trenches down to 60 inches, all the way around the perimeter of the 50×200-foot building. They also dug a trench of similar specifications running the length of the building, exactly 25 feet in from each of the long outer trenches. While this was being done, the dozers were digging out the driveway to the new building and leveling several triaxle loads of stone and gravel brought in to replace the topsoil taken out. This would be critical to allow the cement trucks to gain access to the building.

By three o'clock, a jobsite trailer was brought in and would be the command center for Associated Contractors for the remainder of the project. Shortly after, the rebar was delivered and placed close to the construction site. The Fab 4 watched this carefully orchestrated operation most of the day. There was still an hour of daylight left when the engines shut down as their jobs were completed. They all agreed that after day 1, they had made a wise choice in choosing Associated Contractors, the local company, as their building contractors.

Friday, May 17, 2019, was a beautiful May morning at the farm. Dave, the construction foreman, told Team Johnathan, "We are going to work a couple of extra hours today and work Saturday to complete the reinforcement for the footer. We want to get it inspected early Saturday afternoon. If I call in an order for cement before two on Saturday, they will deliver the concrete Monday morning. I want to get the footer poured ahead of the rain scheduled to start Wednesday morning."

On Monday, May 20, 2019, at 7:30 a.m., two cement trucks, each carrying 11 cubic yards of concrete, arrived at Eagle's Nest. The first truck was emptied by 8:30 a.m., the second by 9:30 a.m. The second truck was still cleaning out its chute when truck 3 and 4 pulled up the driveway. Truck 3 was carrying 11 cubic yards, and truck 4 was carrying 11.5 cubic yards to finish the pour at exactly 44.5 cubic yards. By 1:00 p.m., all trucks had been gone for an hour, and the footer had been completed to specifications. A job well done. The orchestration continued as cement blocks started to be delivered at 2:00 p.m. and continued till 5:00 p.m. The remaining blocks, mortar, and rebar were delivered on Tuesday morning.

Team Johnathan kept the McDonalds informed either when they came to visit the site or at the breakfast or dinner tables. Jackie and Billy had been making contact with all their political friends and contacts. New emails were created and sent to legislators at the state and federal levels explaining their reasons for backing out of the growing aspect of the business and thanking them for their support. They sent all their research to the politicians to help them in making best choices when this all came down, and marijuana became legalized. The number of emails from politicians thanking the McDonalds for their research surprised both Jackie and Billy. They responded in like, offering their input if wanted or needed. The politicians were keenly aware of their state-of-the-art facility that was being built in Crawford County and that it represented an unbiased testing facility for any of their future needs if they entered the marijuana business.

On Monday, as the footer was being poured, Jackie and Billy grabbed each other's hand and began a lengthy walkabout that took them past the pond. They stopped to rest briefly.

While sitting at the picnic table and snacking on granola bars and water, their conversation became emotional.

Jackie began to weep as she told Billy, "Billy, honey, I am ready to have our baby."

Somewhat to Jackie's surprise, Billy replied, "I am more than ready. Why don't you get off the pill, and we can go to your doctor to discuss this option with her? If we can get back in time, let's call her today."

"Billy, I am so glad to hear we want the same thing. I can't wait! I love you, Billy McDonald."

They stood up hugged and kissed and then headed back to the farm, hand in hand, to make a phone call. As soon as they returned to the farm, Jackie called her gynecologist, and to her surprise, an appointment was available the next day at 1:00 p.m.

The receptionist said, "A cancellation has opened the time slot."

"My husband and I will take the appointment."

The next day, the doctor told them, "You will probably need to experience one complete cycle before you will be able to conceive. You are still very young, and you are extremely healthy. You should expect a normal pregnancy and childbirth. Good luck to both of you."

Billy and Jackie simultaneously said, "Thank you."

\* \* \* \* \*

It was Tuesday, June 25, 2019, when shortly after dinner, Jackie and Billy left for a short walkabout. Jackie grabbed Billy's hand as soon as they got up from the dinner table. She held him tight and just listened to her husband, friend, and lover. She would stop every so often and give him a kiss and tell him why she loved him so much.

She knew that this would be the night. They would then move on, and she would do it again and again until they returned to the farm. They returned from their walk at nine and decided to go to bed.

Jackie removed her clothes and headed to the shower as she did every night. Tonight, her stay was extended, and when she returned to the bedroom, she was in her robe, her hair was brushed, her lips glossed, and she was radiant. When she reached the bed, she let her robe slide off her shoulders and drop to the floor and stood before her man as he gazed upon her incredibly exciting body.

She stood there for several minutes, telling him how she needed and wanted her man to make passionate love to her all night long. The more she talked, the more they craved each other's bodies. Finally, she took what she wanted, and as her man penetrated deep into her body, she gasped, and her body shook as she whispered to Billy, "Timing is everything," then conceived their child and went limp.

Although Jackie knew in her heart she had conceived the first time, she continued to make her man happy into the night. She did not tell Billy what she knew and felt had happened deep inside her body. He would know soon enough. Jackie got up early and went immediately to the window. This morning, they were again there. She was not surprised when the eagles seemed to soar in a spirit of love, almost as if they flew as one. Jackie smiled.

Will and Milly joined the Fab 4 for breakfast this beautiful Wednesday morning. They all kicked in and, in no time, had their breakfast made, and all were sitting around the table talking and enjoying one another and their coffee. Milly and Nivea both mentioned how especially beautiful and radiant Jackie looked this morning. She thanked them and smiled, knowing full well the reason for her natural radiance. She was warm inside and out; she knew she would soon be a mom.

# Chapter 19

The meeting scheduled for Wednesday, June 26, 2019, began at 1:00 p.m. sharp.

All were present and accounted for at the table. Guests included the jobsite inspector, the job foreman, the architect, and their state-level political representatives.

Team Johnathan began with a report on the building progress. Johnathan reported, "The block layers had completed their work on June 20, and the project is one week ahead of schedule. The metal roof trusses and crane are on site, and the trusses will be placed on the top layer of blocks within the next two days. Once they are secured, the metal roof could be placed on the trusses, while the plumbers and electricians start placing their conduit and pipes in the subfloor. When that is completed, the massive concrete floor—all 123 cubic yards of it—would be poured. Estimated time of completion of this next segment of work would be three to four weeks depending on the weather. We are pleased with the work of Associated Contractors and glad we chose the local company."

Johnathan nodded to the job foreman.

Jackie stood. "Thank you, Johnathan, for your report, and thank you also, Nivea, for your great work and service to this family. Grandma and Papa, Mom and Dad, I would like to request your help for the next week or so. Could you both keep an eye on things here at the farm? Johnathan and Nivea have been working day and night with the farm, plus the added responsibility of the building project. We would like to give them a week off to celebrate their engagement and have the opportunity to personally share some time with their parents. Billy and I will still be here working on the marketing of the laboratory. That will be taking most of our time, but we will be available to help if something comes up."

All four McDonalds said that they would be glad to step in and help them. Will and Milly agreed that Team Johnathan was long overdue for some R & R. They thanked them for their great work and said they could leave tomorrow morning as far as they were concerned.

"Thank you. You guys are the best. You always seem to know exactly when we need a break," replied Nivea.

William said, "It is so nice that you still included us. We will do what we can to help Will and Milly."

Johnathan and Nivea personally thanked the four senior McDonalds and the two youngest, their best friends.

Since the decision was made to forego the growing of weed as a cash crop, Jackie and Billy continued to be active in local, state, and US politics. They had learned how important it was to know the right people if something needed done relative to their operation on the farm.

They began to pay their dues to the politicians just in case they ever needed them. It was a price worth paying, as they had learned early in their new leadership role at the Eagle's Nest. Thus the presence of their two political guests. Jackie made sure the next thing on the agenda was thanking them both for taking time from their busy schedule to visit the Eagle's Nest.

Jackie looked at their guests, then asked, "Are there any issues any of our guests have to bring forward at this time?" Jackie then looked directly at the foreman and architect.

"Mrs. McDonald, we have no issues that require your attention at this time," replied the foreman.

"Thank you all very much. If all our guests could step outside briefly, we will have our treasurer's report and be with you shortly for a light refreshment."

The four guests waited outside the door as Mr. Moore gave a condensed treasurer's report.

Jackie grabbed hands as a circle was formed. "Bless my husband, this family, our friends, and this farm. Amen. Adjourned." The guests returned to the boardroom, and the meeting after the meeting continued with a light lunch enjoyed by all.

Team Johnathan finished their day and packed with great anticipation for their well-deserved break. They were up and gone by seven in the morning. Will and Milly were both up this morning, early, to have breakfast with their son and daughter-in-law. They enjoyed a relaxing breakfast together, as neither seemed to be in a hurry to get moving. It was one of those rare mornings where conversation was easy and enjoyed by the family. Both couples admitted that they already missed Team Johnathan and that they hoped they had a great time.

Milly called William and Martha at 8:00 a.m. and told them they would be over at 9:00 a.m. to pick them up. William and Martha were still early risers as a result on fifty years of practice. Jackie and Billy were headed to the office and boardroom to put the finishing touches on their marketing campaign. With Team Johnathan gone, they could spread their work out on the boardroom table and leave it out all night. They had been working on it for two months and still needed a couple of weeks to wrap it up. Jackie asked Billy to drive by the construction site before going to the boardroom.

On the way to William and Martha's house, Milly said to Will, "Have you noticed the last couple of days how relaxed and radiant Jackie appears? She is a beautiful woman but seems to be just glowing and more beautiful than ever?"

"Are you thinking what I'm thinking?" asked Will. "You looked just as radiant when you became pregnant with Billy!"

"She has not said anything to me yet," said Milly.

"We will see. It sure would be nice to have a grandchild running around this house and farm. My parents would love to see another generation of McDonalds started before they pass. It would mean so much to them!"

The eldest McDonalds seemed to have been energized as they walked to the car.

"Are you guys ready to inspect the farm, talk to the foreman, and then visit the building site to talk to the architect and building inspector?"

"We can't wait."

They had not had such a busy and important day scheduled on the farm for several years. Jackie and Billy had stopped at the jobsite before going to the boardroom to let the site inspector, architect, and job foreman know that William and Martha would be inspecting the jobsite today and for the next week. They were to make them feel very important.

Jackie looked at the three of them with her soul-penetrating eyes. "Gentlemen, do we understand one another?"

"Yes, ma'am," was their reply.

All three, just like anybody else who came in contact with Jackie, were mesmerized by her beauty. More importantly, they were impressed with her prowess as a business person and knew better than to cross this woman. By now, they also knew she was a lawyer to be reckoned with. A similar conversation was had by phone with the bovine and grain foreman of the farm. Similar responses were heard by both, "Yes, ma'am, Mrs. McDonald. We understand completely."

Wherever Jackie went, she commanded respect! Jackie, now knowing that William and Martha were going to have a great week, settled into her work around the boardroom table. She loved those two and had made a commitment to protect them and their farm long ago. She would not fail!

Everyone made sure that the older McDonalds were shown and given the respect they deserved throughout the week while Team Johnathan was on vacation. Will and Milly transported them in their enclosed Gator accessorized with air-conditioning. This was the first time they had ridden in such a vehicle and just loved traveling around the farm in it. By the time Johnathan and Nivea returned to the farm, William and Martha were keenly aware of all the farm's activities, the work that had been done by Johnathan and Nivea, and the progress taking place in the building of the new laboratory, the farm's newest diversification. They were also glad that Cannabis would not be grown.

* * * * *

The scheduled meeting on Wednesday, August 31, 2019, began at 1:00 p.m. sharp.

Johnathan and Nivea had been back for approximately three weeks. Johnathan started the meeting and was all smiles. "The project is two weeks ahead of schedule and under budget. The roof is completed and ceiling insulation is in place. The electricians and plumbers are a couple days away from releasing their work to the inspectors. Once their work is approved, the floor would be poured. It will be poured the first week of August, rain or shine."

Johnathan and Nivea thanked William and Martha and Will and Milly for covering while they were gone from the farm for ten consecutive days.

Mr. Moore remained seated while he went over his treasurer's report.

He told Johnathan, "I have a check made out to Associated Contractors for the second payout due them. I simply need Jackie's and your signatures."

Billy said, "Our marketing plan is completed. All materials that still needed to be printed were completed and ready to go to the printers. Television promos have been taped and ready to be broadcast. Flyers already have been sent to Pennsylvania Department of Agriculture to be dispersed at all county fairs highlighting the capabilities of the new laboratory."

Jackie and Billy had already attended three of the larger county fairs selling their state-of-the-art laboratory and its capabilities to anybody who would listen. The meeting was over exactly one hour after it started. It was time for a walkabout, and Johnathan and Nivea accompanied them as far as the construction site. They discussed a few building-related issues, and Team Billy continued on their walk. As they returned to the farmhouse, Jackie told Billy she had purchased a pregnancy test kit and wanted to use it when they went to bed this evening.

"Do you think you are pregnant?"

Not wanting to spoil Billy's excitement, she said, "I just do not know. It will be fun to do the test together."

Dinner was early, and all six stayed much longer than usual at the table. When they finished eating and talking, all six started cleaning up the supper dishes and cleaning the kitchen. In twenty minutes, they were done. The two younger couples went for a ride and ended up getting ice cream at Jackie's request.

They returned home somewhat early, but both young couples headed upstairs for two entirely different reasons. It was only a matter of minutes from the time they entered their room before Jackie made a trip to the bathroom. When she returned, she walked out of the bathroom completely naked and walked over to Billy and removed all his clothing.

"Daddy, why don't you make love to your desirable, beautiful, sexy woman? She desires to please you as much and as often as you wish. I love you, Billy. I am so proud to be your wife. I am so happy to carry our child. I can't wait."

## Chapter 20

Jackie awakened early this morning. She was just about to go to the window when she grabbed Billy by the hand and said, "Billy, get up. Come to the window with me. Let's see if the eagles are flying this morning."

They reached the window. Jackie was not surprised when they saw the eagles soaring and diving close to each other as one. They did flips in midair as they carried out ritualistic movements indicative of their monogamous commitment to one another. Jackie's instincts were extremely positive toward these two majestic birds and their presence as they flew with grace, beauty, and love over this special farm called Eagle's Nest.

"Billy, I want to tell everyone of our blessing that God has given us. I want to tell Grandma and Papa first, if it is okay with you?"

"That is a great idea. I will call them now and tell them we are coming for a cup of coffee and will be there in an hour."

When they walked into William and Martha's house, Jackie started to cry.

"Billy and I love one another so much…We have been blessed by God, and we are going to have a baby, your great-grandchild. We wanted to tell you first."

They both were excited, and tears ran down their checks as they hugged their grandchildren and told them they were loved very much. Jackie warmed again.

They finished their coffee and returned to the farmhouse. William and Milly, Johnathan, and Nivea were still at the table talking about farm issues. Jackie and Billy poured themselves a cup of coffee and sat at the table.

Billy told his parents, "Mom and Dad, Jackie and I are going to have a baby. You are going to be grandparents."

Everyone got up from the table and played musical chairs until everyone was hugged and/or kissed. The whole kitchen was filled with love and excitement as they shared in the happiness written on the faces of the expectant parents.

After the excitement of the announcement died, Jackie went to one of her favorite spots—the porch swing—and called her mother and father to share the good news. She had not talked to her mother for a couple weeks, so she was not surprised when she had been on her phone for an hour and a half.

Billy and Jackie called a powwow for high noon in the boardroom with Johnathan and Nivea. A result of one of their walkabouts came the idea they might be better served if Johnathan and Nivea stayed full-time on the building project, with Team Billy taking on the full responsibility of the farm. They presented the idea to Team Johnathan, and they thought it was great. Soon, the building will be ready to receive the laboratory counters, tables, chairs, and equipment, and Nivea and Johnathan needed to be there to organize and oversee to make the laboratory as efficient as possible. They would have to start thinking of staffing the project shortly. Nivea would be the expert in determining specific needs of the laboratory relative to staffing.

* * * * *

The meeting scheduled for Wednesday, September 25, 2019, started at 1:00 p.m. sharp.

Jackie started the meeting explaining the change in roles of both Team Johnathan and Team Billy, and why. Jackie sat as Johnathan began.

"The cement floors were poured the first week in September, as projected. The inside rough plumbing and electrical work is completed and has passed inspection. Doors and windows have been installed. All the interior block walls were painted. The laboratory furniture has arrived, and the workers will soon start to assemble the tables, counters, desks, chairs, and laboratory stools. We will work hand in hand with the plumbers and electricians, making sure water, electricity, and gas go to where it would be needed in the laboratory. All has gone well, and we estimate we are close to three weeks ahead of schedule on this project. This can be attributed to the great work done by the contractors and the weather."

Billy took over, "We had forged ahead with the gas well project months ago, and I am happy to announce, with that project complete and the methane generator, 100 percent of our energy costs have been eliminated in heating all the buildings on the farm. We are also considering, with the help of engineers from Northwestern Rural Electric Co-op and Penn State University, placing solar panels on the roof of the laboratory to make that building less expensive to operate with less of a carbon footprint. We would like to consider wind-generated electricity."

Will stood and congratulated all of the Fab 4 for taking the farm into the next century and the next generation. "You have taken what William and Martha created and transformed it into the farm of the future. There will not be a farm in the state even coming close to rivaling Eagle's Nest in terms of technology, production, and revenue. You are all to be congratulated for your wisdom in decision-making, fiscal responsibility, effort, and work. Job well done."

Everyone in the room stood and applauded their efforts.

The eldest McDonalds' dreams and expectations had been surpassed by the four young people in the boardroom. They knew that all four had made significant contributions but also knew the catalyst was the black-haired woman who was now carrying their great-grandchild. Their life had gone full circle, and with God's favor, they would be given one more blessing before they passed: the honor of holding and welcoming the next generation of McDonalds to Eagle's Nest. They had been truly blessed as they smiled and held each other's hand. The next thing they heard, which brought them back was, "Adjourned."

With Team Johnathan not having to deal with overseeing the farm, their ability to focus on the finish line became enhanced. They could now visualize exactly what needed done to get to the next goal in the construction process. They soon realized that they needed a game plan to go beyond the construction. They would need Billy's and Jackie's input to gain their vision. Their vision would be critical in picking and hiring employees that would represent them and their family. They also needed to find people who could become team members and become a part of the McDonald team. They needed to appreciate their place of work, the history of the farm, and the history of the family that owned Eagle's Nest. They also need to be people of character. It would be a tall order to fill.

One of the many endearing things that Team Johnathan had observed and learned to appreciate about the whole McDonald family was the way they always deferred credit to others. Like the way Will had given all the credit to William and Martha in the boardroom. They also observed that Jackie and Billy never took credit for any of their work and, more often than not, gave the credit to them. They were indirectly learning from the McDonalds something that was not taught at Penn State: leadership and character. They were also learning that you treat people who are important in your life with respect and love. Finally, they learned that trust must be earned. In a very short period of time, they had built a résumé going far beyond their degree work at Penn State.

Johnathan and Nivea retired early for bed that evening. Nivea was in her nightie and Johnathan in his boxers, as they both sat on the bed and talked and reminisced about how lucky they were to do their internship at Eagle's Nest. They had both been exposed to a wide variety of projects that they would never have been exposed to at any other place. They had been treated well and given great responsibility. They had been adopted by this great family and hired to work for them. Their best friends were by their side the whole time. They wrapped their arms around each other and realized that they had also fallen in love and gotten engaged on Eagle's Nest. They gently removed each other's clothing, and Nivea and Johnathan shared their love one more time. They were indeed two very lucky people.

* * * * *

The meeting scheduled for Wednesday, October 23, 2019, started at 1:00 p.m. sharp.

Nivea started by giving the report on the progress of the building. She reported that the installation of the laboratory furniture was just about complete, along with the finishing touches on heating/cooling, electric, and plumbing. They all would undergo final inspection by November 6. A final walk through would take place with all parties involved on the eighth of November, when it would be turned over to the McDonalds. The scientific equipment for the laboratory had started to arrive but would not be placed in its appropriate position until the building was officially turned over to Eagle's Nest LLC. Given any unseen problems, this building and equipment will be ready for business by December 25, 2019.

Nivea reported, "The Fab 4 had been meeting to decide what and who was needed as employees to make the operation run efficiently, effectively, and profitably. We have already received some applications from Team Billy's marketing push at the county extension offices throughout the state and from county fair promotions. A trip to the Penn State job fair would be critical and in the making for November 5 and 6. Johnathan and I have been cleared to make this important event and to represent the farm."

Jackie and Billy also extended an invitation to Will and Milly to help represent the Eagle's Nest at this critical event. "Johnathan and I would appreciate your help. Who better to represent Eagle's Nest?"

"Jackie and Billy have volunteered to do double duty in our absence."

It was Jackie's turn. "Billy and I would like to meet with Team Johnathan and Will and Milly on Friday, at 10:00 a.m., in the boardroom to review our flowchart for the positions we need to fill for the new laboratory. I would like to make sure we are on the same page, especially in the area of high-pay, high-skill positions. Nivea, I want your very specific suggestions and input on this matter as you will not only work there, you will be in complete control of this new facility and its ability to generate income for this farm. You deserve and have earned our trust and this opportunity."

Nivea was shocked, surprised, and thankful for this new responsibility given to her. She then had a flashback to the conversation between Johnathan and her in the bedroom, *Trust must be earned.* She apparently had earned the trust of her best friends. She would not disappoint!

## Chapter 21

The four arrived on the campus of Penn State University around 1:00 p.m. They made their way to the Nittany Lion Inn and checked in for their three nights and four days' stay. Johnathan and Nivea were anxious to find the location of the job fair. They wanted to make sure they knew its location and could arrive in time in the morning to get their booth organized. They also planned on visiting Zeno's to dine and relish the taste of their favorite craft beer. They made their intentions known to Will and Milly and hit the road. This trip to State College was a long-overdue break for Will and Milly. Johnathan and Nivea were getting pretty good at reading their adopted parents. They decided they needed to make themselves scarce for the next three days and nights, except for time spent at the job fair. This, of course, was just fine with them, as they would also enjoy the time together.

The first day at the job fair was exceptional in that they had a lot of interested students in potential jobs at the farm. Most were amazed at the facility and what testing could be done there. The majority were even more amazed that it was part of such a diverse business centered around the farm. Will and Milly, dressed in their Penn State apparel, were the stars of the show as they talked about Eagle's Nest and its family-oriented atmosphere.

The next day was even busier as word of this unique farm spread among the agricultural department. They seemed to be extremely interested in its diversity, its ability to be almost energy dependent, the pure size of the laboratory, and all the state-of-the-art testing that could be performed at the facility and the two McDonalds that helped make it all happen. It appeared that the McDonald farm was the most visited booth in the show. Will and Milly loved the attention they were getting on the grounds of their alma mater. Many of the faculty in the Agricultural Department made a visit to the booth and were likewise impressed.

Team Johnathan had done a fabulous job representing the farm. The video they composed showed both sides of the McDonald farm, bovine and grain. The methane generator and its capabilities were illustrated in the video. The majority of the video contained a start-to-finish production of the new laboratory. The narration by Nivea detailed the overall size of the building, the equipment that it contained, and all the very specialized testing that could be performed on site. William and Milly enjoyed how their two young interns, now employees, talked about family, friendships, and the leadership found in all involved. It was truly a great place to live and work.

The four of them paid special attention to their conversations with these Penn State students, hoping to find the right combination of traits, academics, and personality they felt would work on their farm and in their business. They would take notes, names, email, and phone information if they felt good vibrations from their conversations. This was where they could have used Jackie and her instincts to help them pick who they wanted because they knew her instincts were never wrong.

The Penn State Job Fair was a total and complete success from the standpoint of identifying potential employees to work in their laboratory. It was even a greater success in the pride Will and Milly felt on campus for their farm, family, and employees. In one of their quiet times together in their room, Will and Milly talked about how good they felt about themselves and their part in the success of Eagle's Nest. It would never be spoken again. It was a simple recognition of the other and the parts each had played. They hugged, kissed, and reaffirmed their love for one another.

* * * * *

Breakfast the morning after their return to the farm was filled with a continuation of stories that went on nonstop the evening before. Billy could feel new life in his parents' voices and actions. He continually was amazed at his wife for the decisions she made. It was her decision to send his mother and father to Penn State with Team Johnathan. She always knew what and when something needed done, even in love.

That evening, Jackie treated her man to one of their greatest displays of love ever. In her mind, it rivaled the displays of the eagles. She needed him, and she knew he needed her. It was a combination that Jackie loved to share with Billy. They had gone to bed by 8:00 p.m., and after four repeated exchanges of their love, they collapsed at 10:30 p.m. They both hugged and kissed and fell asleep in each other's arms. As if the night had never existed, Jackie climbed upon her man again at sunrise and thrust herself upon him until they gasped and then collapsed.

Breakfast came early. All six McDonalds and Team Johnathan were sitting around the table, enjoying their breakfast and coffee, heavily engaged in conversation in multiple directions at one time. They were all excited, none more than the two oldest McDonald couples. Today, they all would receive a guided tour of the new laboratory by the contractor and the architect, and if all went well, it would be turned over to the McDonald family.

William and Martha and Will and Milly led the way into the reception and waiting area. A set of doors were opened, and they all entered the laboratory proper. The dividing block wall splitting the length into two 25-foot-wide sections running the length of the building was obvious immediately. The wall not only gave the roof more than adequate support but provided two additional walls for counters from which work could be done and equipment placed. They now had approximately 900 linear feet of counter space from which to work and tables periodically set in the middle of each walkway. At approximately 75 feet and 150 feet, there was a doorway opening leading to the other walkway. Everything was absolutely beautiful, clean, and shiny.

* * * * *

The open house scheduled for Friday, December 20, 2019, at 10:00 a.m., had been planned for weeks now. The local state representative and senator were invited, and they had accepted the invitation. The US congressman for their district also accepted his invitation and presented a check for $2.5 million to Eagle's Nest LLC, from the federal government for the job creation and the assistance the research center would provide farmers in the tristate region. That assistance would be a 10 percent discount on all agricultural laboratory testing run at the center for two years.

What was kept secret to everyone but Jackie and Billy was about to happen. They had covered the left-hand portion of the new building with a tarp for the last two weeks and would not give up their secret. Jackie spoke to the large crowd that assembled for the open house.

"I want to thank you all for attending the official opening of the"—*as she pulled the cord that allowed the tarp to fall*—"William and Martha McDonald Agricultural Research Center."

The large crowd broke into cheers as friends and old neighbors raised their voices in support of the oldest McDonalds. How ironic was it to have such a huge state-of-the-art research center in the shadows of several huge grain silos?

The crowd was lacking children as was suggested for the tour of the center.

"Please ask any questions that you have as we move throughout the center. We will not be in any hurry, so take your time." Everyone seemed to be surprised by how large the building was when they got inside. They were also impressed with the extent of equipment located everywhere they looked.

Nivea told the crowd, "Twenty employees would initially be required to staff the research center, and that number would double in six months. The center would service the tristate area and parts of lower Canada and has the capacity to do the widest range of agricultural testing of any agricultural research laboratory in the United States."

When the tour was over, Nivea told their guests, "If everyone would move to the rear of the building, they would find light finger food, coffee, tea, and water. Any guest wishing to leave the building will need to be escorted out. I'm sorry, but this is protocol for any guests in our building for obvious security reasons."

The event, both inside and outside, had already been recorded on the center's security cameras. The building was a secure fortress. There were several windows to let light in but were composed of ballistic glass, which is relatively impenetrable. All exterior doors were double-thickness steel that opened with key card only. The front was aesthetically pleasing with tall thin ballistic glass windows spaced three feet apart. The front entry door was also double-thick steel. The whole perimeter was lighted and on security cameras. These extra precautions were impressive but were installed primarily to be a system that would allow the center to be considered to test weed if it became legalized.

William and Martha were thoroughly enjoying the open house. It was nice to see friends and neighbors and to catch up on their lives. The smiles never left their faces. It was such an honor to be recognized in this manner by the youngest generation of the McDonald family. They felt honored that Billy and Jackie appreciated the work and effort they had put into the farm. William and Martha knew God's will would be done on this farm. William and Martha were very proud of the work and effort of this younger generation in securing the sustainability of Eagle's Nest for the next, soon-to-be-born generation of McDonalds.

William and Martha had recently met with Mr. White to transfer one of their $2 million in life insurance to Billy and Jackie; the other million would go into the general fund of the farm. They looked at it as an investment in the future. This secret would be well-kept till after their passing.

It was a tremendous public relations day for the research center. Erie, Pittsburgh, Cleveland, and Buffalo television covered the event.

The *Erie Times News*, *Meadville Tribune*, *Pittsburgh Post-Gazette*, and the *Cleveland Plain Dealer* all had writers on the scene describing the testing capabilities of this amazing new research center. Nivea had hired a local photographer to make sure that nothing was missed for posterity or future public relations needs. Stills and videos were taken to document the day.

This PR onslaught reminded politicians at every level to be continually aware of the young couple from Crawford County and the business and political power they were continuing to build and yield. They feared most the dark-eyed, dark-haired beautiful woman with the penetrating eyes named Jackie McDonald. Word had spread of her tenacity and prowess as an adversary. They all knew better than to cross this woman if they wanted to keep their job.

Billy and Jackie boarded their plane the next morning and headed to St. Louis to visit Jackie's mom and dad for a couple of days before Christmas. They would return Christmas Eve Day, and then Team Johnathan would leave for a few days and would return New Year's Eve Day to spend New Year's Eve with the McDonalds. Somewhere in that span of a week, Billy and Jackie would celebrate their first wedding anniversary. They would also celebrate their pregnancy, as Jackie was starting to show signs of a baby bump. She was fifteen or sixteen weeks into her pregnancy.

This Christmas seemed uniquely special for Billy and Jackie. It was their first anniversary, and they were first-time expectant parents. Many of the gifts were special in that they were for the baby. The Christmas tree had blue and pink ribbons mixed in with the clear lights and ornaments. Johnathan and Nivea were moved into Nivea's room, as Johnathan donated his room for the nursery. An entryway between Jackie and Billy' room and the nursery was the only structural modification required to make it workable. Finally, Jackie's instincts told her that this would be the last Christmas to be shared with Grandma and Papa. Jackie's instincts were never wrong.

Christmas and the New Year came and went. Jackie made a conscious effort to spend any extra time she and Billy had with William and Martha. They would go to the house on weekend mornings and eat breakfast with their beloved grandparents. They encouraged attendance at Sunday church service by all six McDonalds and Johnathan and Nivea.

The winter was long, hard, cold, and took its toll on the young and old alike of Northwestern Pennsylvania. Erie, Pennsylvania, had recorded the most snowfall of any city in the United States. Jackie could see the winter was taking its toll on William and Martha. The further along she progressed in her pregnancy, the worse William and Martha became physically.

## Chapter 22

By February of 2020, the William and Martha McDonald Research Center was up and operating at full potential. Nivea's biggest job was continuing to find quality employees as their orders skyrocketed. This outcome was one of many possibilities that Team Johnathan had prepared. Nivea was prepared for anything, as positions were filled from their list of potential employees.

Several times, she thought, *Thank God for the trip we made to Penn State and the job fair.* She was again amazed at the foresight of Jackie to send them with William and Milly. Nivea Anderson proved to be a more-than-capable manager and tremendous leader within the research center, as production from employees was able to keep up with demand. She was pleased with the great job Will, Milly, Johnathan, and she had done screening employees.

One of the smartest things they did at the Penn State Job Fair was recruit a technology specialist by the name of David Long. David's job was to keep their computer programs updated and running. The research center had a multitude of detailed programs to help run and evaluate the different tests done in the center.

Nivea called David Long into her office.

"David, I need you to set up a spreadsheet program that will automatically graph and plot the frequency of every test that we run. I also need it to be set up so any novice can enter the information from January 1 until today by hand. David, I need to know what tests have been done and the frequency of their occurrence. I need to reposition human assets and equipment to become more efficient. We need to generate more work with the same assets."

"That is a great idea, Nivea. I can make it happen. It will set it up so that every computer or laptop in the research center will be able to enter the information. When a test has been completed, it will be so noted on the laptop and automatically, numerically, be transferred to the spreadsheet program so that at any given second in time, you will know exactly what tests have been done and their frequency."

Nivea thanked David and spent several minutes just talking to him about how he was appreciated. She thanked him for his contributions to the center and how much she appreciated the great job he was doing for the center and the McDonald family. Nivea had learned her leadership lessons well from her mentors at Eagle's Nest.

"David, thanks again for all you do!"

"No problem. I will see you around. I can make your request happen by the end of the workday tomorrow."

"Awesome."

Nivea was going to ask Will and Milly if they wouldn't mind helping at the center for a couple of days to enter the data from January 1 to the present. Another lesson learned by the young manager from her mentors: get everyone involved and make them feel they are needed, important, and part of the team. Both Will and Milly worked the next three days until their assignment was completed. Within three days, Nivea had the information she needed, and from that point in time, she had access to it within seconds. She could now make better decisions for appropriation of manpower and equipment within the research center based literally on up to the second data.

Jackie and Billy invited Will and Milly on one of their early morning walkabouts to discuss the future of William and Martha. They all noticed the decline in their health was progressing. Will said to the younger McDonalds, "What do you think needs to be done?"

Billy spoke for the two of them, "We think it is only a matter of time. When one dies, the other will follow shortly thereafter. We also think we need to talk about home health care for the two of them.

They would feel devastated and deserted if they were put in a nursing home. They want to die on this farm!"

"Your mother and I could not agree with you more. We will keep them here! We will make sure the last days of their lives will be on this farm!"

Jackie commented, "It would be nice if they both could live to see and hold the next generation of McDonalds in their arms."

Neither couple was looking forward to what the months had in store for William and Martha. On one of their scheduled morning visits to Grandma and Papa's, they were surprised to see Harry White's car in the driveway. Upon entering the house, an impromptu meeting began.

Harry told Jackie and Billy, "It was the wish of your grandparents to have a living will. They did not want to be kept alive by artificial means. Since you two are the official representatives in charge of the Eagle's Nest, I thought it appropriate that you be the witnesses to this legal document. William and Martha McDonald, being of sound mind, is it your wish that this document become immediately effective?"

They both responded, "It is."

"Jackie and Billy, if you would please sign here as witnesses attesting to the validity of this document, it will become official as soon as I place my notary stamp on it, at the bottom right-hand corner."

All involved parties signed the living will.

"Are the affairs of William and Martha in order?" asked Billy.

"Yes, they are. The will had been changed a few months ago. All of their possessions are to become the property of Eagle's Nest, including their house which had been built for them five years ago. Any personal accounts or insurances were to go in the general fund, with two exceptions. It is my professional opinion that everything is in order."

William and Martha and Jackie and Billy all shook Mr. Harry White's hand and thanked him again for being such a good friend to their family. Mr. White was invited for breakfast, and to everyone's surprise, he accepted. Billy and Jackie cooked pancakes, eggs, home fries, bacon, toast, and coffee. The five enjoyed their breakfast and the company around the table. Mr. White was kind enough to know the situation and to spend some final quality time with his longtime clients and friends. Although never spoken, Jackie and Billy would never forget the kindness and respect shown to their grandparents by Mr. Harry White. They now understood why this man represented Eagle's Nest and would continue to do so for as long as he wished. He was a man of character.

* * * * *

The William and Martha McDonald Research Center was operating at full capacity with forty employees by mid-April. They were not only getting work from their agricultural friends from across the tristate area but were starting to get requests for DNA testing from law enforcement agencies as an independent testing site. They would soon need to restrict their clientele or add on to create more space for their DNA testing. They had not even gotten to the point of possibly testing the quality and potency of weed produced by the growers of pot for medicinal and/or recreational use in the state. This issue would have to be considered at the next board meeting.

The meeting scheduled for Wednesday, April 22, 2020, began at exactly 1:00 p.m.

Noticeably absent from the meeting was William and Martha McDonald. Jackie opened the meeting with a prayer, "Dear God, please be with William and Martha, thy good and faithful servants. Protect them and keep them close to you in their final days. Please comfort them in the knowledge they will soon be in thy presence, and all their pain and suffering will be gone. When their time comes, welcome their souls into thy household, and strengthen us who are left behind to live our lives to be worthy of you. Amen."

It was obvious that Jackie was in her last weeks of pregnancy. She was huge and even struggled getting out of her seat to say the prayer. Jackie and Billy had not told anyone at the table the sonograms indicated twin boys. It would remain their secret until birth.

Johnathan and Nivea gave their reports. Nivea's report contained important decision-making material for the farm. She explained, "We are already at maximum capacity at the research center. If this business trend continues, we will net $750,000 in the next year from the research center-generated business alone. This is $250,000 higher than projected originally. We are starting to get many requests to generate DNA test results as an independent facility separate from the police and governmental labs to ensure nonbias reliability of results.

"I would like to remind you that we have not even begun to test marijuana from growers for medical or recreational use. I need the direction of the McDonalds to proceed. I personally feel that we could reproduce this building and have it at full capacity within six months, sooner if the state legalizes marijuana in one form or another."

Quiet fell upon the room. No one had expected this research center to take off like it did. Will spoke, "What is your opinion, Nivea? You run the center."

"Mr. and Mrs. McDonald, if you so choose to reproduce the current building, I feel that one year from its completion, it would net this farm another $750,000 and possibly more if we start testing state-authorized weed. We would surely be able to secure higher profit margins testing that product for the growers. Growers would like the idea of placing the sole responsibility on anyone other than themselves. Mr. and Mrs. McDonald, Jackie and Billy, my question is, how much is too much? I would ask what would William and Martha suggest we do? In closing, with everything that is going on around here, with William and Martha's health and Billy and Jackie's pregnancy and imminent birth of their child, we continue to think about this and return to it in another two or three months. I would suggest also, if we would decide to move forward, I would need an assistant, and the best person would be Johnathan because of his background.

"I think you have all seen we work very well together. If that is what you would so choose, then a replacement for him on the farm side of the business would be required."

Billy said, "Nivea, your suggestion is well taken. We will return to this issue at the July meeting, and in the meantime, we can all give this further thought."

They formed the circle, holding hands, and Jackie said, "God bless my husband, this family, our friends, and this farm. Amen. Adjourned."

## Chapter 23

Jackie checked on the eagles every morning. She had noticed that the eagles had completed their nest in early March and that the female was spending more time in the nest. She wondered if she had laid eggs in the nest. It became very clear she had laid eggs when the female left, and the male immediately took her place keeping the eggs warm in her absence.

Jackie went to bed early feeling very uncomfortable, and her instincts told her that this was the night. She lay down on the bed, and within one hour, she told Billy that their time had come. She was ready to deliver their babies. Will and Milly, Johnathan and Nivea followed Billy and Jackie to the Meadville Medical Center. Within an hour after arriving, Jackie was giving birth to their first child, and within a few minutes, their second child was born. The deliveries went smoothly, and mother and babies were fine.

The babies were in their incubators when Billy told Will and Milly as he pointed, "The one there is your grandson…and the one there is your other grandson."

Will and Milly were so surprised, astonished, and thankful for this blessing that had been bestowed on them. Johnathan and Nivea could not believe what their eyes were beholding—two tiny brand-new human beings, perfect in every way. They hugged their best friends and his parents as they remained in awe of these two creations of God. They returned to Jackie's room and waited their turn to give hugs and kisses to the new mother of twin boys.

Twin boys born to Jackie and William McDonald III on May 15, 2020, at 10:15 p.m., at Meadville Medical Center, Meadville, Pennsylvania. Two days later, they were to return home. Jackie was adamant that they first had to stop at Grandma and Papa's so they could see and hold the boys.

Everyone else had their chance to hold the boys, and now it was their turn. With the assistance of Will and Milly. the boys were taken into the house. William and Martha were in their hospital beds brought into their bedroom to make them more comfortable. Jackie and Billy carried their boys into the bedroom.

"Grandma and Papa, look what Billy and I have for you today!" They both knew what this meant as tears immediately rolled off their checks. "These are your new great-grandbabies. Billy and I had twin boys three days ago. Would you like to hold them?"

Martha's and William's tears turned into smiles as the boys were brought to them in bed.

They talked to the boys as they held them in their arms. In a very low soothing voice, Martha sang a lullaby to the boys, who opened their eyes and gazed upon their great-grandparent's face and seemed to smile before closing their eyes again. There was not a dry eye to be had.

Jackie said, "Papa, we have to go home now and get our babies settled at the farmhouse."

Billy and Jackie took their boys from their grandparents as Martha whispered, "We love you. Thank you."

Jackie whispered into Grandma's ear, "The eagles have returned." Grandma smiled and closed her eyes. She would not open them again.

The hospice nurse told the family that it would not be more than a week for both of them. Their organs were beginning to shut down, and they would be made comfortable. She told them it was a good thing they came today. She did not know how much longer they would have known what was going on. Everyone thanked the nurse for her excellent care given to the two special people lying in those beds. Jackie felt a personal feeling of calm come over her as they left, knowing she had fulfilled her obligations to these two beautiful human beings.

The next week was a bag of mixed emotions as everyone was celebrating the birth of the two new McDonald boys and, at the same time, watching the death of the two oldest McDonalds. It was truly a dichotomy of emotions. On May 27, 2020, both William and Martha McDonald expired sometime between 2:00 and 3:00 a.m. When the nurse checked on them, they apparently had died holding hands. They must have known when it would happen. She did not disturb their final act of love. The family was called, and all arrived by 3:30 a.m. to be together as family. They did not disturb their last act of love. They would leave that to the funeral director, who would be arriving shortly.

Once their bodies had been taken, they returned to the farmhouse, where they were joined for breakfast by Johnathan and Nivea. Will and Milly filled the early morning conversation with funny stories about William and Martha that had them all laughing. They would be missed, but their lives were to be celebrated. Will and Milly needed to go to the funeral home and make the unique arrangements to bury both parents. Billy declined and opted to stay and help Jackie with the boys. Team Johnathan would tend to the business of Eagle's Nest in everyone's absence.

Billy did not know his grandparents knew so many people. The viewings were packed and extended well beyond the scheduled viewing hours. The funeral was moved to the church to better handle the expected huge crowd. Will did the service for his mother and father. His focus was on the strength of character and work ethic exhibited by his parents. He gave numerous examples of their willingness to help a neighbor or friend in a time of need. He also referenced their deep love for God Almighty.

He closed by reading the twenty-third psalm and said, "It is now time for William and Martha to spread their love and goodwill in heaven and fly with the eagles."

\* \* \* \* \*

One week later, Mr. White met with the family in the boardroom for the reading of the last will and testament of William and Martha McDonald. Mr. White provided copies to everyone in attendance for the reading. Present were the two McDonald families and, at the request of Mr. White, Johnathan and Nivea.

"The McDonalds each had a $2-million life insurance policy. In William's case, the designated beneficiary is the general fund of Eagle's Nest LLC. In Martha's case, the beneficiaries are William 'Billy' McDonald and his wife, Jackie Mc Donald. Their remaining personal assets in the amount of $200,000 was bequeathed to Will and his wife, Milly McDonald. The house built for them five years ago is to be provided to Johnathan Best and Nivea Anderson for their cohabitation at no cost to either of them for rent, utilities, or taxes. This will be considered additional compensation for their exceptional service to this family and this farm, as long as they remain employees and/or married. Are there any questions?" His condolences were again made known before he departed.

Johnathan and Nivea expressed their appreciation to the family for the gift they had just received from William and Martha. They thanked the family for their trust in them as friends and employees. They would continue to be worthy of their trust and friendship and would never let them down. They excused themselves and returned to work. Jackie also excused herself to return to her newborns.

Billy, his mom, and his dad sat at the expensive table in complete silence for several minutes. As they sat there in silence, they were all thinking the same thing. They were hoping they could live up to the examples set by William and Martha. Billy finally said, "I will sure miss those two. I hope I will be able to emulate those two great individuals."

His mother said, "Son, you already have." They joined hands and asked for God's continued blessing on this family and this farm. They also thanked God for the blessing of Johnathan and Nivea in their lives.

\* \* \* \* \*

The scheduled meeting on Wednesday, June 24, 2020, started at 1:00 p.m. sharp.

Mr. Moore started the meeting with his report, "Billy and Jackie, you now have assets over $5 million in accounts in your name. The trust in Billy and Jackie's control to be used at their discretion for the continuance of the Eagle's Nest has assets of over $8 million. The general fund of Eagle's Nest LLC currently has a balance of over $3 million. This increase is due to some payments for a drawdown of natural gas and from increased revenues from the research center. Ladies and gentlemen, this business is in sound financial shape. The building you have been considering meets the depreciation and tax benefits that I was going to suggest needed addressed."

Billy told Johnathan and Nivea, "Proceed with this new project as quickly as possible. Johnathan, we would appreciate a trip by you to Penn State to locate our new overall manager of the farming side of this business. Find us the right woman or man for the job. By now, you know what we need and want in an individual."

Jackie then told Johnathan, "You have the authority to hire this person if you find what we are looking for. If you are not happy with the choices, fly to Columbus, Ohio. Ohio State has a good agricultural school. You have one week tops. You will leave tomorrow morning for State College, accompanied by my dad, who will help you find the right person. It is important that this gets done. Nivea, we'll need you to keep one building operational while we build another right beside it. Billy will take your place until you get back. We need two things, and we need them done as soon as possible, and we are entrusting both to you. Find us a manager, and build us a building."

Johnathan responded, "Jackie and Billy, we will get it done."

Will and Johnathan returned back to the farm in three days, having hired the farm manager. She would be arriving in two days.

# Chapter 24

On June 29, 2020, the new farm manager appeared on the scene at Eagle's Nest. Upon her arrival, the McDonald family, along with Johnathan and Nivea, welcomed Judy McBride into the boardroom and to Eagle's Nest. Also present were Mr. White and Mr. Moore.

Jackie spoke first, "My name is Jackie McDonald, and this is my husband, Billy McDonald. We both own and operate this farm. We are so glad that you have joined our team. You must be quite the special person if you were chosen by Johnathan and my father to oversee the farming aspect of our business."

Jackie completed the introductions.

"Thank you all so much for such a fine welcome. My name is Judith or Judy McBride. I would prefer Judy. I will require some time to get adjusted and find my way around this beautiful farm. I will work closely with your employees and foremen to make this farm as productive as possible. I am here at your pleasure. I will do the best job I can for this farm, for this family, and for this business."

Jackie's instincts kicked in almost immediately, and she got a very good feeling about this girl they would call Judy.

Jackie's instincts were never wrong. Jackie told Judy, "You will stay at the farmhouse for the first month until you get comfortable with the farm and your job. After the first month, it is your option. While you are here, your room and board will be provided. You have the rest of the day free to get settled into your room. Breakfast is at 6:30 a.m. Milly will show you to your room. Your salary will be $80,000 per year. Do you have any questions?"

"No, ma'am," was her response.

"Johnathan and Nivea, you have received Grandma and Papa's new home to use as long as you both work here, at no cost to you. Billy and I have increased your combined salary to $200,000 per year starting today. You have both been loyal friends, supporters of this family, and improved the revenues of this farm substantially. Congratulations to you both for a job well done. Billy and I cannot thank you enough!"

They grabbed hands to form a circle. "God bless my husband, this family, our friends, and this farm. Amen. Adjourned."

\* \* \* \* \*

At 6:20 a.m., Judy walked in the back door, ready to eat her breakfast. Billy asked Judy, "Where have you been?"

"I went out to the bovine area and introduced myself to the foreman. He explained a lot to me as we did a few jobs that needed done. I will catch the grain foreman after breakfast."

Will and Milly had gotten up to share some time with the new employee. Billy, Johnathan, and Will decided that they would cook for the girls today. As they placed the food on the table, Judy was already impressed with her new family. When the food was gone, the coffee drank, and the day's assignments were done being discussed, all three men cleared the table, cleaned the dishes, put them away, and allowed the four women a chance to talk. Billy could overhear Jackie mentioning Tyler and Thomas to Judy. Judy smiled at the mention of the twins.

Judy asked if she had access to the four-wheelers for business use. Will said, "You have access to anything on this farm for business use and most anything for personal use."

Nivea told Johnathan, "I have work to do in the research center today, getting the ball rolling on the building.'

He said, "I will contact the architect and Associated Contractors. I will tell them we want another building just like the last one, except we want a ballistic glass walkway connecting the two buildings. I will inform Mr. Moore and Mr. White of our plans. Security must be a major concern in the new building. If we accept the contract to test state-produced weed, it will need to be a very secure building."

They all rose, and their day began. Nivea to the research center, Johnathan to the phone. Jackie would escort Judy to the grain area of the farm and continue with a four-wheeler tour of the McDonalds' holdings, including a tour of the research center.

Jackie told Judy, "Any testing you need done, simply let Nivea know, and it would receive priority status for completion. You will need an office, and you can take over Will's office next to the boardroom."

"Are you sure Mr. McDonald will approve?"

"You need an office, and he knows it. He has already given his consent."

Billy would stay until Jackie returned to watch Tyler and Tommie. Watching his boys would be the best part of his day.

By the end of July, the earth had been moved, the footer dug, the rebar set, and the footer poured.

The scheduled meeting on Wednesday, July 22, 2020, began at 1:00 p.m. sharp.

Judy was about to witness her first official board meeting. Milly was absent from today's meeting. She had the pleasure of watching her two favorite grandsons.

Jackie began, "Mr. Moore, you can give your report at this time."

"Billy and Jackie, your personal accounts are now over $5 million. The account that you two supervise for the growing and sustaining Eagle's Nest has risen to $8 million. The general fund budget that pays the bills for the farm has risen to $5 million due to increased revenue from the research center and drawdown on natural gas."

"Thank you, Mr. Moore. Mr. White, have you anything to offer?"

"Yes, I do, Jackie. The $1 million in life insurance money that you and Billy received as beneficiary of Martha McDonald has been deposited in your personal account. The $1 million that William bequeathed to the operating budget of this farm has also been deposited in the appropriate account. The $200,000 bequeathed to Will and Milly has also been deposited in their personal account. Copies of deposit slips and account numbers and balances are shown on this paper. Thus, the increase in the value of those two accounts of $1 million each and the increase in the other of $200,000."

"Johnathan and Nivea, do you have anything to report?"

"Yes, we do, Jackie!"

Nivea began, "We are experiencing no problems with the testing and/or the results of our testing. We are operating at full capacity and have been doing so for several months now. All is good in the research center. If all continues, our projected net revenues will easily reach $750,000. The new building is moving ahead as fast as humanly possible. The footer has been dug, reinforced, and poured. The masons will move in next to lay the blocks for the walls. It will be close, but this building should be ready to move into by New Year's Day 2021.

"I have heard rumors that a possible vote might be taking shape on legalizing marijuana in the near future. The bill is still in committee but is expected to emerge sometime in the next year. It is my opinion that we pull our political allies in here and find out what they know. They owe us big-time. It is time for us to collect. I will need to know before we place equipment in the new building."

Jackie responded, "Very good report, Nivea. We have all thought about this for some time. This is a very important decision for the research center. There may be public relations issues if it gets out we are testing marijuana for the state. Harry, what is your opinion on this matter?"

"There are no legal ramifications if you decide to test state-sponsored marijuana."

"Harry, do you have a business opinion?"

"From what I have noticed, your testing business is spreading its wings into new territories almost every month. As long as Nivea and Johnathan can continue to produce quality test results, your business will continue to grow. The DNA testing business is skyrocketing. I personally have no issues with you testing marijuana. I think the issue is how fast can you grow? How fast can you find the quality employees you will need? If you decide to test state-sponsored marijuana, I think you are looking at a third building. I also believe that your net revenues from that business could reach 1.5 million per year on its own."

Mr. Moore spoke next, "I do not see how you can lose financially. The two issues are finding out what the legislature has in mind for us and if we go to three buildings and test weed. Can we find quality people to do the testing? I am sure the state will have guidelines for hiring that we will have to follow. Do you want state inspectors and state employees snooping around in your buildings?"

Jackie concluded, "Let's call another meeting in two weeks. That will give everyone time to think this out. Billy and I will pull in the politicians for that meeting and find out what they know and tell them what we need done. Like Nivea said, they owe us big-time. Judy, any comments?"

"I have a couple of things to discuss. Both foremen are doing an excellent job. Your employees are good people and hard workers. I have had difficulty finding service records on much of the equipment. I would like to ask permission to service every piece of equipment on this farm. Harvest on the grain side will be taking place in a few months, and I do not want to lose a piece of equipment on the premise that it should have had the oil changed, and it hadn't."

"Judy, when Jackie and I took over the farm, I asked a similar question to the people in this room. They told me the same thing I am about to tell you. You do not need our permission. You were the most skilled and talented of all applicants. Just do what you feel needs to be done, and I'm sure we will be pleased with you in every way. We have complete faith in you and your abilities to run this farm at peak performance, or you would not have been hired. Money is not an issue as long you can justify how it is being spent."

They held hands and formed a circle. "Bless my husband, this family, our friends, and this farm. Amen. Adjourned."

Judy stayed and made herself available for the meeting after the meeting to socialize with her new family. Jackie informed the girls that dress for the next meeting was businesslike attire.

The very next morning, every piece of equipment was identified by type, make, and serial number. They were all listed on a spreadsheet, with maintenance requirements listed for each piece of equipment and vehicle. A space was also provided for date accomplished and date for next maintenance due. This list was given to both foreman and told it was their responsibility to make sure maintenance was done on every piece of equipment on their side of the farm.

They had three weeks to complete their task. They were to fill out a report every time maintenance was done and turn it in to Judy, plus mark it on their spreadsheet. If outside mechanics were brought in to work on any piece of equipment, there was a form that they needed to fill out and were to hand it personally to Jackie and discuss what was done before they were to leave the farm. If maintenance was not done when due, Judy's laptop would let her know.

Judy was amazed at the faith this family put in her ability to do her job. She could now better understand what she was told by Mr. McDonald about the leadership on the farm. Judy also noticed that most of the talking and apparent leadership within this meeting was done by the women. She was not a feminist but was impressed by how involved women were in the decision-making process in this successful business operation. She had also observed the unselfish teamwork that she knew could not be found in any other work environment. The financial stability of this business impressed her most. She now understood why diversity was so important in the business of farming or in any business. She had found her dream job and was surrounded by great people. She would not disappoint this family, this business, or this farm.

# Chapter 25

The scheduled meeting on Wednesday, August 12, 2020, began at 1:00 p.m. sharp.

Both invited representatives arrived fifteen minutes early and joined the men that were already seated at the table. At exactly 1:00 p.m., the three women walked into the room and apologized for being a bit late. They looked beautiful. Hair hanging and brushed, gloss on their lips, their eyes highlighted. Their clothing was appropriate but somehow provocative and intriguing at the same time. The three women were absolutely gorgeous. Their guests' eyes were fixed on them and followed them to their seats.

The other two women found their seats while Jackie remained standing. The McDonalds normally did not discuss their finances in a meeting where guests were present. Jackie made an exception, as these boys needed to be reminded not only of the McDonalds' political prowess but that they had money to back it up.

"Mr. Moore, could we please have a brief accounting of our business?"

"Yes, Jackie. You and Billy have an excess of $5 million in your personal account. The trust you control has an excess of $8 million. The general fund has just over $5 million."

"Thank you, Mr. Moore. Harry, do you have anything?"

"No, ma'am." The two employees knew exactly what just went down.

Jackie looked at their guests. "Gentlemen, thanks for making the trip to Eagle's Nest. Do you have any information for us relative to the vote on legalizing marijuana?"

The senator spoke first, "We think that a vote will be had sometime in the next year."

Jackie told them, "Our research indicates there are presently enough votes for this bill to pass. What have you heard?"

"We would agree with your research."

"Gentlemen, we are currently constructing a second building here at Eagle's Nest and considering the possibility of a third. We need to know if we have a chance at getting the contract for testing the marijuana long before the vote takes place. We are talking an expenditure of over a million dollars for that third building. We will be adding 40 more jobs by February and, if this contract can be assured, 40 more jobs within a year. I want you to make this your number 1 priority, if it is not already. It is critical to the economic improvement of this region. It would be nice if you could hear me and Billy giving you the credit for 120 new jobs at Eagle's Nest next election.

"Honestly, if you can't get this done for your constituents, I'm not sure you deserve to represent this area. I will call both of you in two weeks, and you can update me as to our chances. Gentlemen, do we understand one another?"

"Perfectly."

"Please keep us informed, and if you need any help, just let us know. Thank you for your time."

They knew better than to challenge this woman personally or politically. They got up from their chairs on their cue and left the room. Judy could not believe the tenacity of her boss in dealing with the politicians.

In two weeks, Jackie called the office of her state representative and state senator. Their responses were identical. "Your influence on all eighteen of our state's US congressmen must be complete. They have all encouraged every state legislator to vote for a bill that would forward all marijuana testing to the William and Martha McDonald Research Center in Northwestern Pennsylvania. Their reasoning is it would be the safest way of keeping unbiased and consistent testing for all product grown in the state and eliminate any influence by the bad guys. They have verified the character of everyone at the Eagle's Nest and the William and Martha Research Center as beyond approach. It appears your political influence is greater than even you may have surmised."

\* \* \* \* \*

The meeting scheduled for Wednesday, August 26, 2020, began at 1:00 p.m. sharp.

The foreman from Associated Contractors and the architect were invited to the meeting and arrived fifteen minutes early. Jackie stood and began the meeting, "Judy, do you have anything to offer?"

"The grain foreman and I have been starting to check the crops more closely as we get closer to harvest. All equipment on the farm has had a complete maintenance review. A record has been established by type, make, and serial number for all equipment and vehicles owned by the farm and recorded on a spreadsheet."

"Thank you, Judy.

"We have been assured that the William and Martha Research Center will be awarded the contract to clinically test all marijuana samples for all marijuana grown in the state for purity and potency for a period of ten years. We have also learned that the vote will take place in the next year, and it will pass. The expected net revenue for the farm will be at least $3 million. We will need another building built ASAP. When these three buildings all get functional at the same time, our net revenues per year will be in excess of $6.5 million dollars from the research centers alone.

"Our architectural firm may begin the planning process as soon as possible, and our friends from Associated Contractors can start planning for building number 3 as soon as the drawings get approved. Do either of our guests have any issues with moving forward ASAP?"

"No ma'am, we are good to go."

"Can we be ready to move dirt in one month's time?"

"Normally I would say no, but the drawings are so similar I don't see a problem."

"Let's make it happen. Gentleman, we will need that building ready to go by March. Is that an issue we need to concern ourselves with?"

Both men simultaneously answered, "No."

"Nivea and Johnathan, it is your turn."

Nivea stood. "We currently are planning the number 2 building will be identical to building 1. It will be connected by a twenty-foot ballistic glass walkway located at the middle point of the two buildings. We intend to use that second building to be able to test everything with a focus on DNA. This is the fastest-growing portion of our business. It will generate more money than the other testing, with the exception of marijuana.

"The third building will be used solely for marijuana testing. It will be big enough to handle everything we need to do. There will only be twenty-five state-certified growers. We should be more than able to handle the state's demand in this ten-thousand-square-foot building.

"This building will more than pay for itself, so I suggest we keep it completely separated from the other two buildings. The other reason is I cannot imagine that the state will allow the testing facility to connect to another building."

Johnathan stood. "Either you or Billy can find out what the state has in mind as far as who we can hire and who we cannot and if they have their guidelines formulated yet. I am sure they will be as closely checked as educators. We need to know this when we begin to recruit for employees to work in this isolated building. I would also suggest another recruiting trip to Penn State and Ohio State to start the search for another group of special employees. Our architect needs to inquire if there are any special building requirement for our testing facility. Finally, we need to meet again in two weeks. There is much meat on this bone we decided to chew."

Jackie thanked Nivea and Johnathan for their great work together. "Billy and I will follow through on the state requirements that exist or could exist in terms of the hiring process. The architect will follow through with the state and report to us at the next meeting. Since the last trip was so successful, is there any reason Johnathan and Nivea and William and Milly could not attend Penn State and Ohio State to represent Eagle's Nest at the fall job fair at both schools?"

All four smiled and said they would love to go again. Billy was already on his iPhone and had the dates for both fairs so plans could be made and scheduling could occur. "Mom, would you take care of getting us registered and the lodging for both trips?"

"I will call today."

"Thanks, I will give you the dates when we are done today."

Nivea continued, "For the sake of Mr. Moore and everyone present, I have devised a projected net revenue of building 1 to be $1.25 million a year, building 2 to be $2 million a year, and building 3 to be $3.5 million per year. Ladies and gentlemen, that adds up to an additional net revenue for Eagle's Nest Farm of $6.75 million a year in just three years' time. I rarely swear, but that is pretty damn good!"

Billy stood. "We have come a long way, and everyone has worked very hard to accomplish great things for Eagle's Nest LLC. Everyone has shown great teamwork to achieve our goals. The number 1 goal was to take this farm and this business into the next generation, and we have accomplished that goal. Johnathan and Nivea deserve a great deal of credit for much of what has been accomplished, and all of the McDonalds—past and present—appreciate all your efforts. If William and Martha were in this room today, they would be so proud of everyone. We must continue to pursue our goal, as there is much yet to do. I am confident that we will continue to work together.

"I would like to remind you all, first and foremost, this is still a farm. We feel we have hired the best possible person to continue to make our farm more efficient and profitable. Judy, thank you for all your efforts to keep this farm the most efficient and productive farm in the state. Mr. Moore and Mr. White, we thank you for all your work, support, and confidentiality in all the transactions you carry out representing the interests of Eagle's Nest.

"I would now like to thank my mother and father for all their work over the years that has put us in a position to be able to do these great things for the farm. Finally, I would like to thank my beautiful wife and lifelong partner for all of her efforts. Without her, none of this would be possible."

Everyone in the room stood and applauded Jackie, a sign of their love and respect for this amazing woman. Billy closed, "God bless my wife, this family, these friends, and this farm. Amen. Adjourned."

Will and Milly provided a light snack and drink for after the meeting. It was obvious that the meeting after the meeting was getting longer and longer since Billy and Jackie had taken over. There was more to discuss as the business became more involved. It was a great time to communicate, ask questions, ask opinions, and to become better friends. Mr. White and Mr. Moore had their meeting after the meeting after the meeting by Mr. Moore's car.

"This organization is absolutely amazing. I cannot believe the maturity of this group of young people. The leadership exhibited by Billy by his deflection of credit to all his employees and family is rare indeed in the business world. I have never seen anything like it in all my years as a lawyer."

Mr. Moore responded, "I do believe they appreciate us and feel we are a part of their team. I do not get this feeling with any other clients. See you later, Harry."

"Okay."

## Chapter 26

Christmas 2021 was very special in the McDonald household. The boys would experience their second Christmas. They were one year and seven months old now and enjoyed ripping the paper to get to their Christmas presents. It was so perfect. Will and Milly enjoyed their grandsons very much, especially at Christmas. They even volunteered to watch the boys Christmas Eve so Billy and Jackie could enjoy their third anniversary together.

They opened up the door to room 205. It was the exact room they had two years earlier on their honeymoon. The first thing they did was to commence taking a walkabout to get some fresh air and to talk. They loved to walk and talk. On their way back to the room, Jackie tested the waters.

"Billy, I would like us to have another baby. What do you think?"

His response surprised Jackie. "Can that happen tonight?"

"It is perfect timing if you so wish to try tonight!"

"I want a baby too. I was going to talk to you about it tonight. It is still early. We have lots of time before we have to go and eat."

Jackie moaned, "Baby, it's been too long!"

When they returned to their room, Jackie told Billy to undress, and she would meet him in bed. She went into the bathroom and returned in a see-through nightgown. As she walked toward Billy, she lost the gown. She stopped in front of the bed and let Billy take in everything she was about to share. Billy could see that childbirth had not affected her innate beauty. She was as beautiful as the first night she removed her clothes for him in her apartment. Her body was firm, her muscles defined, her breasts shapely, her stomach flat, and no gain or loss in weight. She was still a wonder to behold, and he loved her more than ever.

After several hours of lovemaking and all their needs satisfied, Jackie whispered to Billy, "I am pregnant."

"How do you know?"

"My instincts tell me so, and as you well know—"

Billy finished, "Your instincts are never wrong."

"Billy, it is going to be a beautiful baby girl. Her name will be Cameron. She will be more beautiful than me, smarter than me, and have more drive, tenacity, and prowess than I ever had. She will soar with the eagles and take this farm to even greater heights than even we could have imagined. She will be an amazing girl and woman. She will meet and marry a man more wonderful than you, if that is possible."

"That sounds amazing and something to really look forward to."

Billy had never questioned the how or the why behind Jackie's instincts. All he knew was that they were always right, and he had no reason to doubt this most recent revelation of his now-pregnant wife. He simply gave her a kiss, told her he loved her very much, wrapped her in his arms, and they both drifted into their dreams of the new baby girl to come.

# Chapter 27

Building 2 was now running at full capacity. DNA testing had increased to three-fourths of all business coming out of building 2. Johnathan and Nivea's projections made two years ago were right on target as far as projected revenues for that building. Building 3 was also up and running. Fortunately, the security that was in place for building 1 and 2 was more than adequate to meet the state standards for the building that would test the marijuana. This saved the farm thousands in architectural fees. This was another big score in Nivea's and Johnathan's résumé. They had been batting one thousand in all the major projections about the construction and operational business of all three buildings.

The biggest hassle for everyone in building 3 were the state inspectors. They were in the building at least once a week and sometimes more. They were just doing their job but often got in the way of the employees doing their jobs. The additional money derived from building 3 had built-in additional costs as a consequence of the inspectors. Fortunately, this had also been accounted for by Team Johnathan.

The meeting called for on Wednesday, January 26, 2022, started at 1:00 p.m. sharp.

Jackie turned it over to Nivea. "To all my dear friends and adopted family, I have nothing but good news to report. All three buildings are working at capacity. We have not experienced anything unexpected in the operation in building 3. All our employees were handpicked as a result of our previous trips to Penn State and Ohio

State. The state inspectors are a pain in the butt, but they are very satisfied with our procedures and results. It is important to keep them satisfied.

"The revenues that I estimated a while back are right on and will show in Mr. Moore's report. Mr. Moore, where are we?"

"Billy and Jackie, $6 million, trust fund $9 million, farm fund $6 million. These numbers will continue to climb over the next nine years. This reflects only building 3 up and running for two months."

Jackie asked, "Are you and Johnathan able to stay on top of all three buildings?"

"It is starting to get more difficult. I would think it wise to start to train one of our group leaders to be able to supervise all three of our buildings. Billy, I would also like to make you somewhat familiar with the operation so you also could fill a spot if necessary during an emergency."

"Count me in. It makes sense to me. I will make myself available Monday, Wednesday, and Friday in the morning. Plan the training of the new supervisor based on my schedule. You guys need to hire a new employee to replace the group leader you move up to building supervision. It seems to me this should be a priority. That will give us three supervisors for three buildings. Raise Judy's and his or her salary to $90,000."

Nivea and Johnathan both thanked Billy for the extra supervisor and how quickly he solved their issues.

"Jackie and I decided on one of our walkabouts that we want to have a Fourth of July picnic for our staff and family. We would like it to be completely outsourced except for the beef that we will provide. I want it to be such that they move in the day before the Fourth and move out by noon of the next day. I want the organizers to set up games for the children and provide people to supervise the games and help watch the kids so parents get some time to themselves. I want a professional ground and aerial fireworks display for the kids and their parents. I want tents, chairs, tables, the works. I do not want alcohol on the property. Please make sure all employees are made aware of this in advance. It will not be tolerated. This will be a family picnic.

"We have no concern for cost. Our employees have done an amazing job for this family and this farm. Jackie and I want them to know how much they are appreciated. Mom and Dad, can you organize this, make the contacts, and make this happen?"

"Consider it done, son."

"Mr. Moore, would you please contact our payroll department to produce a five-hundred-dollar check to be given to every employee on the Fourth of July as a gift from Eagle's Nest Farm LLC? Mr. Moore and Mr. White, we would be honored to have you and your families as special guests of the Eagle's Nest Farm.

"In the envelope with the check, I want to include a thank-you note to all employees, from Will and Milly McDonald. I would also like you to hand deliver each. Dad and Mom, will you do this honor for Jackie and me?"

"It would be an honor, and thank you both for the privilege of representing the farm in this manner."

"Dad, we are in this position and able to do these things right now because of the years of effort by Grandma and Papa and you and Mom."

They formed a circle and held hands as Billy said, "God bless my wife, this family, our friends, and this farm. Amen. Adjourned."

Although everyone was very busy doing things for the farm, there seemed to be a calmness within the leadership. Everybody loved their jobs and wanted to be here at this place, at this time. It was an exciting time! As everyone was leaving, only one person felt the eagles flying high above in protective flight over the farm. Jackie looked up and began to wonder if the spirits of Grandma and Papa flying with the eagles above had increased her unique sense of instinct and her ability to feel the future before it occurred. They were, in fact, soulmates, and she was the gift they had prayed for every day.

When the crocuses and daffodils finally overtook the snow and started to bloom, spring had arrived in Northwestern Pennsylvania. The robins soon followed as the days became longer and the air warmer. An unusual sound was heard this spring above the chorus of the birds. It was a sound that had never been heard on the property. The sound of two McDonald children playing at the same time.

Tyler and Tommie would spend most of their daylight hours traveling about the farm with either their grandparents or their parents. They were most often seen on or in some form of a four-wheeler, although now they could dismount and walk. Often, they could be seen holding their grandparents' hand going in and out of barns enjoying the animals of the farm. They would soon form a bond with their grandparents and this farm that would last their lifetime.

Johnathan and Nivea would be married in August. They wanted to be married at Eagle's Nest, but Nivea's mother, Mrs. Anderson, would have none of that. Spring passed to summer, and Johnathan and Nivea were married. Summer passed to fall, and Jackie would soon have their precious baby girl.

## Chapter 28

Jackie's water broke, and the McDonald caravan headed to Meadville Medical Center and none too soon. Within a half hour of arriving, Billy and Jackie's baby girl was born. Cameron Jacklyn McDonald entered this world at 3:15 p.m. on Sunday, October 2, 2022. William and Milly held their granddaughter, and each could feel how special this girl would be as soon as they held her in their arms. She was adorable. Her hair was black and curly, and she had a remarkable resemblance to her mother.

As Cameron grew older, her mother could see exactly just how special she was becoming. She noticed things that others could not. Cameron Jacklyn McDonald was becoming a true force of nature right in plain sight of her grandparents and parents on Eagle's Nest Farm. Her mother knew that whatever she chose to do, successful people would follow. Her instincts told her so.

As the children grew, it was Jackie who taught them of the struggles and contributions of past McDonalds and the heritage that was being passed onto them every day of their lives. First and foremost, she taught them what a very special man they had for a father. She talked to them of their great-grandma and papa. She explained how Grandma had named the farm. She taught them the sacrifices of their grandparents. She taught them of her unique and unexplainable ties to the eagles. She taught them of their strong faith in God. She explained her special relationship to Great-Grandma and Papa.

The children grew to respect their heritage and love for their grandparents, parents, and Eagle's Nest. They also learned what a very special person they had for a mother and her contributions to the farm. These stories were always taught by their father and reinforced by their grandparents. The theme of all the stories told always ended up centering around one theme: love!

Will and Milly did not have to wait to be great-grandparents like William and Martha to know that Eagle's Nest Farm would be in capable hands. Cameron, along with Tyler and Tommie, would take the farm into the next generation. Jackie realized all her inner feelings that she shared with Billy the night Cameron was conceived had come to pass except one. Jackie could feel the eagles soaring majestically above the farm and would look for them every morning out her bedroom window. The eagles had, in fact, returned to Eagle's Nest for good.

Johnathan and Nivea followed the birth of Cameron with the birth of their own child. It was rare to see one without the other three during the summer. They all had chores and responsibilities in the grain and bovine areas and in building 1 and 2. It was important to their parents that they not only learned responsibility and hard work but also how those areas of the farm operated. There was no admittance to building 3 under any circumstance.

All four were taught right from wrong. They were taught the importance of dependability and character in one's life. The four of them were all top-notch students. They loved school and loved to learn. They all were taught the importance of learning at home, and all four were very inquisitive. They were taught of God's influence on the farm. Cameron just stood out as being exceptional in all she did.

Cameron was developing into a beautiful young woman. She was very friendly and social, but as she grew older, her mother taught her well in the ways of the world and to protect herself and her body until she felt she had found the man that would love her forever. Cameron never struggled with this, as her mother explicitly explained to her the night she gave herself to her father and why. She explained what a gentleman he was even when faced with her partially naked body all evening. Cameron also loved to take showers to relax.

\* \* \* \* \*

All four youth on the McDonald farm attended the alma mater of their parents.

Cameron had pursued a law degree at Penn State, while Joseph was pursuing a degree in biochemical engineering. They were both finishing their sixth year of schooling. It was 2046, and the Nittany Lions had a great team.

Cameron's phone displayed Joseph's face. "Hey, Cam, do you want to take in the game today? I have tickets."

"Sure, I'm all caught up on my work, and I would love to go with you."

Cameron and Joseph had grown even closer in college than they had been at home on the farm.

"I will pick you up at 11:30 a.m., and we can walk to the stadium."

The game was an exciting three-point Penn State victory. They took their time walking home, and as soon as they left the stadium, Cam grabbed Joseph's hand as they walked back to her apartment.

She invited Joseph up to her apartment, as she so often did when they did things together. She told Joseph she wanted to get a quick shower. Joseph knew this was not unusual behavior for her. Cam liked her showers. In twenty minutes, Cam returned to the room in a full-length see-through nightgown.

"Joseph, I think I love you, and I want you now. I want you to be my first."

"Cam, I know. I love you too. I know how you feel about this. Are you sure?"

Cameron loosened the tied bow at the top and the gown as it slid off her shoulders. She grabbed Joseph's hand and led him to her bedroom, where she removed his clothing. This was the first for both of them. They could not keep their eyes off each other's beautiful naked bodies. She was the most beautiful woman Joseph had ever seen. She looked directly at his penis and was surprised at the size of Joseph's manhood. When she looked up, Joseph was looking directly into her eyes.

Cam smiled. "Take me."

She laid him on her bed and lightly stroked her man with her fingernails and carefully prepared to mount her man. Cam was an innate lover like her mother. She instinctively made love beautifully and completely. She had a tremendous sexual appetite like her mother. She looked forward to the sensations she was about to experience with Joseph.

She was surprised by how moist she had become and how firm her nipples were as she slowly started to descend upon him. She was completely aware of what she was doing, her environment, and all the feelings she had waited so long to feel. When she made contact, she easily slid down on him. She slowly moved on him, up and down, moaning and groaning at the beautiful new sensations she was experiencing deep within her body for the first time. She could feel the full length and girth of her man stimulating her into a sexual frenzy. Her body was on fire.

The moans continued, but the sounds became louder as she thrust herself on him over and over, pushing him deeper into her body. She began to quiver inside and out. She could feel this glorious man against her on the inside. With her last final thrusts and her quivering tissue surrounding her man, she could feel him start to contract and to release deep within her body. Her nails dug into his chest, and she screamed his name out loud, over and over.

Cameron was not only the most beautiful woman on campus, she was also the most beautiful lover on campus. God had blessed Cam and Joseph in their physical lovemaking. They repeated this act of love over and over till they both collapsed in exhaustion.

Cameron thought to herself, *Love like this should not be humanly possible*. She just smiled to herself with her good fortune, kissed and told Joseph that she loved him. Cameron's sexual desires went off the chart after her first time with Joseph. Joseph was a gifted man and could satisfy Cameron's needs on all levels. Jackie had explained her own sexual desires to Cameron. Cameron and Joseph, like Jackie and Billy, became gifted lovers. They both had the tools necessary to satisfy each other's sexual desires.

Cameron and Joseph had never seen each other naked. When they arose and got into the shower, it was like they had seen each other's naked body their whole life. They were very comfortable with the other's naked body. It felt completely natural to the both of them. Cameron, though, could not take her eyes off of Joseph's penis. She looked forward to taking it again and again. It was an early evening of firsts for the two young lovers.

Cameron said to Joseph, "I have loved you for a long time." She whispered into his ear and nibbled on it as she asked her man for more. She would not be denied! When they got out of the shower, they dried each other's bodies, got dressed, and went into the living room.

Cameron told Joseph, "I love you very much. I cannot believe what a beautiful lover you are. I also cannot believe all the feelings, sensations, and emotions that I feel when you are with me. I will love you for the rest of my life."

Joseph responded, "Cam, I believe you know that you are a very beautiful woman. You are a very special person. You have always been a kind, thoughtful, caring, and loving person with all you come in contact. I am so lucky to be your man and your lover. I will love you and be faithful to you forever. A lot has happened here today, but one thing I know for sure is I want to share the rest of my life with you. Will you marry me?"

"Oh my god, Joseph, of course I will marry you."

"Cameron, let's go tomorrow and pick out your rings."

Cameron, for the first time that evening, began to cry as she reached for her man and gave him a kiss and a long hug. Cameron had a very warm feeling stream throughout her body. Her instincts told her that she had just made love to the man she would love forever. Her instincts of late were never wrong. "Joseph, let's go for a walkabout."

The evening was still young as they began their walkabout. Cam asked Joe, "When would you like to get married?"

"As soon as possible. And you?"

"As soon as possible also"

"Joseph, are we crazy doing this so soon?"

"Probably."

"Sounds good enough to me."

Cameron said to Joseph, "Let's get married tomorrow after we get our rings."

"Deal! Boy, I had no idea when I got up this morning, I would make love for the first time in my life, and I would do it several times to my favorite girl in the whole world, propose to her, have her accept, and marry her the next day. This is the best day of my life."

Cameron, being the practical one, asked, "What about our parents?"

"We will call them after we get married. If they want, we can do it again on the farm."

## Chapter 29

"Cameron, what do you want to do with your life?"

"Why do you ask?"

"I have been thinking about creating a world-renowned think tank on the grounds of Eagle's Nest Farm. I do not want to work in a college laboratory doing research all my life. What a great thing we could create! The greatest young minds in the world located in one place, working on solutions to a wide variety of issues including political, agriculture, scientific, environmental, industrial, transportation, religion, and others. Clients would pay money to have many of the brightest young people on the planet working to solve their problems. It would be an amazing environment to organize, supervise, and administer."

"Joseph, it sounds intriguing. I think the two of us need to give it more thought before we present this proposal to the board. It would be an endeavor that we both could work on together. It would challenge the intellectual side of our being. Our grandparents and parents could get involve by getting our representatives politically engaged. It would be rewarding to create the environment within which problems are solved."

They returned to Cameron's apartment for the night. They removed their clothes and slid under the covers. They snuggled up to their mate and dreamed of the days that would be shared together.

The next morning, they both got up early as usual, showered together, got dressed, made breakfast, and headed to the jewelry store to buy their rings. Cameron found the rings that she loved.

Joe also found what he wanted. Cameron thanked Joe for the beautiful engagement and wedding rings. Joe got down on his knees and officially proposed in the jewelry store. This beautiful young couple, who loved each other very much, headed out the door to locate the justice of the peace to repeat their vows and legally be declared husband and wife.

They walked out of the local justice of the peace office as husband and wife and returned to Cameron's apartment to call their parents.

First, Joe called Johnathan and Nivea. "Hey, Dad, what are you guys up to?"

"Just finishing some work in building 3."

"I have some exciting news to share with you."

"What would that be?"

"Cameron and I got married today. We love each other very much and have for several years. We want to spend the rest of our lives together. We felt we could not go another day not being married. I love you. Please give Mom the news. We will make a trip home this weekend to share this with you and Mom. Please do not tell Jackie or Billy because Cameron is going to call next. I love you."

"I love you, too, Joseph."

"Hi, Mom, I love you. How are you and Dad?"

"We are fine, and you?"

"I'm calling to let you know that Joe and I got married today. We love each other and want to spend the rest of our lives together. We could not stand another day not being married. I'm sorry I did not let you know sooner."

"Cam, honey, I have known for a very long time that you would ultimately be Joseph's bride. I am very happy for the two of you. May God bless your lives together."

"Thanks, Mom. We will be home this weekend to share time with you guys. Give my love to Dad. Tell the boys. I love you, Mom."

"I love you, too, honey."

Cameron and Joseph left State College at 7:00 a.m. They arrived at Eagle's Nest around 11:30 a.m. The house was full of family, all wanting to see the newlyweds. Will and Milly, Billy and Jackie, Tyler, Tommie, Johnathan, and Nivea were all present and accounted for.

Jackie had baked her daughter and new son a wedding cake. Milly made the punch and provided the ice cream. They had a nice reception for the new couple.

Tommie, the wise guy of the family, said, "You're not pregnant, are you?"

Cam responded with a no and landed a solid punch to her older brother's right arm.

Joseph and Cam both felt satisfied that their parents were okay with their marriage. Both parents always knew these two had loved one another for some time now. The new couple made plans for their new house that would be built for them as they finished their last year of schooling. They put a great amount of thought into its location before Cam would release the plans to have it built. Although they had not decided on their plans for the think tank project, they both agreed to position their new home close to where they would build the project, if approved by the board.

\* \* \* \* \*

The Bests moved into their new home immediately after their graduation from Penn State.

The meeting scheduled for February 16, 2045, started at 1:00 p.m. sharp.

Cameron stood first and asked for the floor. Tommie said, "Go ahead, sis."

"Joseph and I have a proposal to bring forward. We have devised an idea over the last year that we feel will not only make Eagle's Nest known nationally and internationally, help many people, and make this business even more diversified and lucrative. Projected revenues on the bottom end are 25 million per year and on the high end 100 million per year.

"We believe we can create a think tank housed on this property. A minimum investment of $6 million would be required. The dividends on that investment will be huge. The concept being, we search out some of the brightest young minds in the world and invite them to work with other brilliant minds to solve some of the world's biggest problems. Businesses and governments would pay us huge fees to engage these minds to solve their problems. We get paid up front."

Tyler interjected, "Cam, the money in the operating budget of this farm is close to $40 million. If you and Joseph think this will fly, I'm with you one hundred percent."

Nivea responded to her daughter in-law, "Years ago, we had the crazy idea to grow marijuana as a cash crop and that evolved into the William and Martha McDonald Research Centers and has provided tens of millions in dividends to this farm. Johnathan and I say go for it."

Jackie and Billy were amazed what their daughter and new son had planned. They felt it was especially worthy of their unique and special talents. Both Jackie's and Cam's instincts felt very good about this project, and their instincts were never wrong.

The final vote was Tommie's, and all he said was, "That's some serious cash."

Cameron closed, "God bless Joseph, Grandpa Will and Grandma Milly, Mom and Dad, Eagle's Nest-, Johnathan and Nivea, Tyler and Tommie, our friends, and this farm. Amen. Adjourned."

After the meeting, Cam was on the phone to contact their architect from Pittsburgh. They responded and said they would have Elizabeth there in the morning by 10:00 a.m. That would make for a long night for Cam and Joseph to prepare for this introductory meeting with the architect. They decided to go back home and get some sleep for a couple of hours before they started their all-nighter. After a shower, they returned to their extra-large kitchen table, put on full pot of coffee, and began the tedious work of determining the needs of their $6-million building.

The architect arrived exactly at 10:00 a.m. Elizabeth was invited into the boardroom. Present were Will and Milly, Johnathan and Nivea, Jackie and Billy, and Cam and Joe. The architect explained what features would be built into this special and expensive building based on its high-security demands. It took care of all the issues they had written on their tablet the night before. Cam described to

Elizabeth she wanted a large open space that would be surrounded by the building. The architect knew exactly what she wanted. Cam told her she wanted the exterior well landscaped but nothing too close to the building. They would also require language interpretation equipment so all could communicate. The initial plans were approved. The total project cost reached $15 million with the projected cost of equipment necessary for these brilliant men and women to do their jobs. The additional money was not an issue to the budget of the farm.

Dirt started to move by the end of April 2045. The new building was huge. Expected completion was April 2047. Cam called on her mother and father several times as it came time to market this plan. They had two years. Jackie and Billy learned years ago the importance of maintaining influence on their political friends. Their influence grew as their wealth grew. It was time for a trip to Washington, DC. Calls were made, and a large audience of politicians from throughout the nation were to gather on April 24 in the nation's capital.

The trip was made by Jackie, Nivea, Joseph, and Cameron. The featured speaker was obviously going to be Cameron. Cameron, much like her mother before, had learned early that the power of intelligence combined with beauty could be deadly on a predominantly male audience. Jackie, Nivea, and Joseph would help Cameron answer questions after the presentation.

The United States representatives and senators that were in attendance were treated to many things that night. They were exposed to the greatest single human force they had encountered in their lifetime. They realized this woman was a force of nature and would have to be dealt with now and in the future. Men and women alike were mesmerized by the intellect and beauty of these impressive woman. More importantly to Cameron, they were intrigued by Joseph's idea. They were impressed that the McDonalds had already broken ground on this $15-million project. Cam pushed hard for assistance to help them acquire all the equipment necessary in the various fields to satisfy this collection of young men and women who would solve many of the problems of business, industry, agriculture, and science.

Several in attendance whispered, "What a great presidential candidate she would be."

Within the next six months, grants from various United States agencies such as Agriculture, CDC, NSF, NOAA, NASA, and many others started pouring into Eagle's Nest Global Research Institute. Within six months, they had a start-up budget of $100 million and climbing. The board had agreed early on that no monies would be accepted from businesses and special interest groups to avoid any appearance of collusion.

* * * * *

The meeting scheduled for May 15, 2047, began at 1:00 p.m. sharp.

Today's meeting would take place in the Global Research Institute.

Cameron took charge. "Joseph and I want to thank you all for your help and assistance that has allowed this magnificent building to be completed on time and on budget. We will open with an operating budget of nearly $250 million, thanks to the generosity of many government agencies. As you tour this building and observe its beauty and serenity, please also note the tens of millions of dollars' worth of equipment. Everything you see inside and out is completely paid for. The 15 million originally budgeted has been returned to the operating budget of the farm. We are standing here today, in this unique building, debt-free. Again, we could not have done this without the help of everyone. I know if Great-Grandma and Papa were here today, they would be extremely proud of the way this family works together as a team.

"Tomorrow, we will have a tour of this building by several US senators and representatives, along with various heads of governmental agencies that financially contributed to this project. Invitation only. I apologize for all the extra noise as vehicles come and go throughout the day and aircraft will be landing and taking off from our runway. The next day will be an open house for any interested community members. There will be two tours—one at 12:00 p.m., and one at 6:00 p.m.

"You will notice today that one wing is dedicated housing. It will contain twenty separate large bedrooms, a cafeteria, a large gaming room, a well-provided exercise room, and a large common area. Our clients will live on site and have access to all work, activity, and relaxation areas 24-7. Our waiting list is long, and we have chosen our first twenty clients to arrive July 1, 2047. Our waiting list is also long for people wanting to spend large amounts of money to be provided our unique services. Johnathan and Nivea, would you please supervise the day-to-day operations of this new building?

"Mom and Dad, would you please be in charge of all incoming and outgoing correspondence and make necessary contacts and arrangements for the institute? Each team will have their own office and secretary. We will meet every Monday, Wednesday, and Friday at 8:00 a.m. to make sure we all are on the same page so something does not sneak up from behind and bite us in the butt.

"Joseph and I will deal with all the problems that will go on when they arrive. We will determine what topics will be worked on and the corresponding billing. This is a cash-up-front business. If they do not want to pay, we move on to the next customer. It is absolutely critical we produce results. We will administer all aspects of the actual think tank.

"Tyler and Tommie, is everything going well on your end? Are you both able to stay on top of things?"

"Yes, sis," they both replied.

"Good, if you need anything, take care of it. I love you guys. You boys do the work of this business, and we all appreciate your efforts. Generation after generation have been reminded that this business is, first and foremost, a farm. The other businesses can come and go, but this farm is here forever. It is the roots that have always supported the tree. Thanks, boys."

"You are very welcome, sis," replied Tommie and then Tyler. They both appreciated their sister's comments.

The next day was May 16, 2047. Eagle's Nest was alive with activity as VIPs converged on the farm. The parking lot at the institute was full of vehicles, and private jets were lined up and parked well off the main runway near the McDonald's private hangar. Cam was dressed in casual clothing, as were most of their guests. At her side was her mother and Nivea. The three women would be welcoming tour guides. Cam was there to answer the technical questions.

Every guest was totally blown away by the complex. Halfway through the tour, they entered the living and dining area where refreshments were offered, and questions were asked and answered. The second half of the tour focused on all the laboratories and equipment for each technical area. It was truly an enlightening tour, and all in attendance were more than impressed as to how their money had been spent. The general consensus was that these women had it together. All knew before they arrived that they wanted to meet and talk to the youngest and most beautiful as she was truly the unexplained force that drew everyone she came into contact with into her force field of influence. Cameron did not disappoint.

Buses transported any dignitaries that wanted to view the methane generator and the William and Martha McDonald Research Centers, now with five buildings. Again, *amazing* was the word that was most often heard as they passed through the barns and the five testing centers. Many were surprised at the collection of solar panels that covered all five roofs of the testing centers. This attention brought smiles to the faces of both Tyler and Tommie.

None of the politicians had ever seen anything that matched this farm. Prior to departing, all of the VIPs were drawn to Cameron by an unknown force they could not explain, to thank her for her most gracious hospitality. The day's requirements for Cam had finally been reduced to zero. She could not locate Joseph, so she hopped on a four-wheeler and headed to her beautiful new home. Joseph had been working more than anyone to secure a successful open house for the institute. When Cam entered their home, she found him in bed, sleeping. She quietly entered the bathroom and closed the door so as not to wake him. She would let him sleep. She set her alarm early, as she had plans for her man in the morning.

To Cam's surprise, Joseph was already awake and grabbed his wife's hand and said, "I want you."

They proceeded to repeatedly meet each other's needs until they were both satisfied.

"What a way to start the day," said Cam. She winked at him and said, "I will catch you later."

Early that morning, when Joseph headed to the institute to prepare for today's two tours, Cameron went in search for her mother for coffee and conversation at the farmhouse. She walked in the back door and said, "Hello? Mom?"

Jackie and Milly said in unison, "Come in."

Jackie welcomed her daughter, "Good morning, honey. How are you today?"

"I'm fine. Good morning, Grandma. How are you?"

"I'm fine, thank you. How are you today, sweetheart?"

"I'm doing awesome. Can a girl get a cup of coffee around here?"

Grandma Milly responded, "Get a cup out of the cupboard, and I will pour your coffee."

"Thanks."

Jackie said to Cam, "What brings you to the farmhouse so early this morning?"

"I was hoping to get some coffee and that we could talk."

"What's on your mind?"

"Is it possible that I could have picked up this instinct thing from you? I often have this feeling that comes over me that makes me feel like I know how something is going to turn out before it does. It's not logical. Mom and Grandma Milly, every VIP, representative, and senator made a special point to come to me before they left yesterday to thank me for our hospitality. Many of them mentioned that they felt an unknown force that drew them to me. What do you think is going on?"

"Honey, I do not know."

Jackie said, "I do not think you know what I'm about to say. Cameron, on that night your father and I conceived you, when we finished making love—over and over I might add—I told your father that I was pregnant. I knew instantly. It was the very first time we made love that night. I told him we were going to have a baby girl by the name of Cameron. I told him she would be more beautiful than her mother. I told him she would be stronger, smarter, and wiser than her mother. I told your father she would be more tenacious than her mother and have the prowess of a tiger. Finally, I told your father that you would be a force of nature that would have to be reckoned with in your lifetime. I would also assume you and Joseph have an extremely active sex life. I would bet to the point of not being able to get enough of each other."

"Mom."

"Cam, you fit all of the above. Ask your dad to verify if you do not believe me. That's what I know. This is what I believe. I formed a tremendous bond between your great-grandmother and great-papa. I believe they soar over this property protecting all below.

"The last thing I said to Grandma McDonald was the eagles have returned. She smiled, closed her eyes, and never opened them again. I believe the souls of your grandparents fly with the eagles. I can feel them when they are in the air. I do not even have to see them to know when they are there. I believe they talk to me without speaking. I believe on December 25, 2020, the night you were conceived, they were speaking to me. Cameron, I really believe, because I have been told, you are, in fact, a force of nature. You are a very special woman, my dear sweet Cameron, with very special powers at your disposal."

"Mom, why did you wait so long to tell me this?"

"Because you never asked. I knew when you would ask, it would be the right time to tell. You see, honey, you are now the woman who carries the torch of this family, and you have been given special skills to do great things for this family and the world, if you so choose. Use your own wisdom as to when or if you tell your husband. He deserves to know what you are capable of doing once you figure that out yourself."

"Mom, can you and Nivea run the morning tour, and I will do the second? Thanks for the talk. I need to find my man and give him a hug and a kiss."

"I hear you, sweetheart."

# Chapter 30

July 5, 2047, was the official opening day for the Eagle's Nest Global Research Institute. Cameron and Joseph had the twenty interns broken down into four groups of three and two groups of four. Each group worked on a different problem to solve. What they didn't know was the original problems were only to seek out which people could be best placed with others to receive maximum reward for time input. This was a great opportunity for these interns. Sometimes these special people work best alone. The most important thing to find out was which in the group were a total waste of time and money and get rid of them ASAP. Jackie and Cameron often worked together with their special innate instinct detective devices to save time.

By the time the first week ended, they had lost five interns. They quickly reorganized into their best combinations of five groups of three. It was time to get serious about solving the problems put before them. Each group of three would work on their own problem and one day out of five with another group of three on the other group's problem, hopefully giving the insight and perspective of the outsider looking in. Cameron and Joseph did a great job keeping the interns on track, and Jackie had the uncanny ability to shed light on every group's problem as she moved about between the groups daily. With her uncanny perspective and input, the institute was shedding new light on old problems as its reputation was improving almost daily.

As their reputation improved, so did the quality of candidates they received to evaluate for intern positions. They also got better at playing the game and more easily could determine which prospective candidates would survive as quality interns. Normally this type of environment would be cutthroat and ego-driven, but again Cam, Jackie, and Nivea had a calming effect on the whole institute. Prospective interns started wanting to come to the institute to work based on what they had heard about the management of the building.

Good news travels fast, as more quality interns applied, and the number of contracts attained also increased dramatically. The Eagle's Nest Global Research Institute was gaining international acclaim as one of the foremost research and development centers in the entire world. The only difference: these were young kids manning the stations. Everything Jackie and Cam touched turned to gold. This also included the McDonald family, which was their most cherished success project of them all. The Global Research Institute had netted the farm 85 million in year 1 and could conceivably double that in year 2.

Even with the success of the institute, Cam remained humble and most certainly loved her man more than ever. At the end of this day, Cam and Joseph changed their clothes at the institute and took off on a walkabout before riding their four-wheelers home for the night.

Cameron could see why her parents loved their walks. It was exercise but more importantly a time to talk and share.

Cam said to Joseph, "Have you given any thought to having children?"

"All the time."

"I think tonight would be a great night to conceive, if you so choose," said Cameron to her husband and lover.

"Cam, I have been ready for two years."

The night was a special night. Cam and Joseph engaged in lovemaking many times. Their bodies were as one as they repeatedly made love throughout the night, enjoying their partner's special gifts. Each time was special, but Cam knew she had become pregnant that very first time. She would explain in the morning; for now, she would enjoy her man's love.

* * * * *

It was time for another morning meeting with her mother. "Mom, can you come over to the house for coffee and conversation?"

"Sure, honey."

"You can bring Grandma if you like. I do not know why, but she needs to be here."

Jackie and Milly arrived ten minutes later. Cam poured the coffee.

"I'm pregnant."

"When?"

"Last night."

"Are you sure?"

"As sure as your daughter can be when she is told."

"I am so happy for you two."

"Is it a boy or a girl?"

"Girl."

"Are you sure?" asked Milly.

"As sure as I can be," replied Cam. "She will have a force much greater than yours and mine combined, Mother. God, William, and Martha have plans for their great-great-granddaughter. She is going to be a magnificent girl and woman. She will be ravishingly beautiful. She will be extremely intelligent and caring. She will be compassionate to all mankind. She will lead, and people will follow, drawn to her by an unknown force. I do not know how. She will not stay at Eagle's Nest as an adult. She will be a force in this nation and in this world. Mom, remember when you used to tell me how you could feel the presence of Great-Grandma and Papa?"

"Yes."

"In her absence, she will be felt in the hearts of all remaining on the farm just as if she were there. She will marry. I do not yet know his name. Mom, he will be special, if you know what I mean. Please do not tell any of this to Papa, the boys, Billy, Joseph, Nivea, or Johnathan. I will tell Joseph of my pregnancy tonight when we go to bed. We can announce to all in the near future. Well, what do you think, Grandma Milly?"

"I do not totally understand. I know I love you two girls very much. I know your mom is special in many ways. I know you are even more special than your mother. I know you both see and feel things the rest of us cannot. I do believe Angela will be even more special, and she will draw millions to her."

"Oh my god, Grandma Milly, you just named my baby."

Milly could feel the presence of William and Martha flow through her body as she instantly felt heat. "She will truly be angelic, Angela Best."

Cam said, "Angela Best it is."

Jackie interjected, "You know, it seems that our lives were pre-ordained, all leading to the birth of this special girl." Jackie grabbed the hand of her daughter and her mom as they formed a small circle.

Cam spoke, "God bless Joseph, the love of my life, Great-Grandma and Papa, Grandma Milly and Papa Will, Momma and Daddy, Nivea and Johnathan, Tyler, and Tommie. God bless this farm, and God bless this life that is growing in my tummy. May God walk with her all the days of her life. Amen."

"Amen."

"Amen."

\* \* \* \* \*

All was good on the farm. The grain and bovine portions of the business were doing exceptionally well, thanks to Tyler's guidance. All five buildings of the William and Martha McDonald Research Center were functioning at full capacity, turning out close to $15 million in net revenues per year. Cam and Johnathan's showcase building the Eagle's Nest Global Research Institute was contributing a minimum of $100 million net a year. All remained uniquely humble from top to bottom as the farm's net worth grew from $35 million, when Billy and Jackie took over, to over $250 million now that Cam and the boys were in charge. They were acquiring more money than they could ever spend. Cameron projected a net worth of $1 billion within five years.

Jackie grabbed Will early and said, "Ride with me." They went out and saddled their horses and rode off. Jackie rode Bullet. Their final destination was Cam and Joseph's house.

"Why are we stopping here so early in the morning?"

"Because your granddaughter and I need to talk to you."

They entered, and Cam was sitting at the table, waiting.

"Morning, Papa."

"Is something wrong?"

"No, we just need to talk."

Jackie spoke first and told her dad all her experiences in their entirety, from the first night she made love to Billy to the present. Then Cam began her story about her instincts. She told him about all the guests that came to her before they left and how many of them told her that there seemed to be this force that drew them to her before they departed.

She then proceeded to tell him, "The night before last, Joseph and I were making love and I knew the instant I conceived, and it would be a girl. It would be a very special girl."

"Dad, do you know anything about Grandma and Papa you need to tell Cam and me? If it is on a need-to-know basis, now is the time. We need to know. This all started as soon as I started dating your son. My daughter, your granddaughter, is going to give birth to a very special baby in nine months. She will have powers much greater than Cam and me combined. She will draw millions of people to her for guidance and leadership. It almost seems that Grandma and Papa connected to me, and then God chose me and all my female offspring to be and do special things in our lifetimes, and each generation is given a larger task and greater powers."

"Faith," he said. "This, I know! My parents had faith in God. Do you really think your Papa and I, two humble, hardworking human beings, built Eagle's Nest into what it is by ourselves? It could not be done in two short generations!"

Jackie said, "I questioned the instant success years ago."

"Your Papa's faith was strong, and he received blessings and help in decision-making from God Almighty. He also knew that Grandma Martha and Milly where stronger, smarter, and their faith was unrelenting. He and Martha prayed every day for an intelligent, beautiful, powerful, woman with unrelenting faith and passion to come to Eagle' Nest. Jackie, when you arrived, they knew their prayers had been answered."

"Papa, is that why we girls have this unrelenting passion for our man?"

He smiled and said, "I believe so, my dear sweet baby."

Cam smiled and said, "Thank you, Papa. I needed to know why. Grandma Milly named my baby already. Angela."

"I know, honey. She told me. It is and will be very appropriate. It is a beautiful name."

"Thanks, Papa, I love you."

"Jackie, I believe they still pray for you. I think they still watch over you, and now Cam. I think there are special things God can do for those who love him down here on earth. Martha, Milly, you, Cam, and now Angela are five of his special people on earth. Jackie, I believe that you have done such a beautiful job in God's eyes that he has entrusted more power and responsibility to your female offspring. Cam, that would be you. Cam, you have also been an amazing human being, and God is pleased with you. I believe he will now entrust more responsibility and power in Angela. She will be a goddess. God's love, power, and wisdom will flow through here veins, and she will radiate God's love wherever she goes. I only hope I live to see it. That's all I know."

"Thanks, Dad, Cam and I appreciate you giving your explanation. We love you very much."

His two beautiful women walked over and gave him a hug and a kiss.

# Chapter 31

Joseph and Cam did not realize when they conceived Angela that her birth date would be close to Christmas Day 2050. That day would also be Billy and Jackie's thirty-first wedding anniversary. Cameron elbowed Joseph in the arm at 1:15 a.m., Christmas morning.

"Joseph, it is time to deliver our baby."

Joseph started the car, and by the time they were ready, so was their car. On the way to Meadville, Cam called both sets of parents and told them they were on their way to Meadville. By the time they arrived, Angela Jacklyn Best had arrived at 2:45 a.m., weighing in at seven pounds and twenty and a half inches long.

She was in her incubator when her guests looked upon her. She had Joseph's brown-to-sandy hair color. Her eyes were as dark as her mother's. The Bests could not get over the natural glow on their granddaughter's face. Jackie and Billy knew a talk would soon be in order with Johnathan and Nivea, their best friends in the world. She knew it would go just fine.

Joseph took his mom and dad into the room as the McDonalds passed to allow Johnathan and Nivea the first opportunity with their new granddaughter. When Jonathan and Nivea returned, Nivea said, "She just seems to be a very special girl."

Billy and Jackie knew exactly what they were holding and that she, in fact, would be very special. What a special Christmas gift God had given both families.

Cam and her baby were both doing fine. The doctor told her she was scheduled to go home with her baby on the twenty-seventh.

The whole caravan departed together after a short visit with Cam. Mother and baby were doing fine, and both needed some well-deserved rest. Cam's brothers would visit their sister later in the day.

Everyone was invited to William and Milly's house for New Year's Day. Jackie had decided it was going to be the day of the unveiling. By the end of the day, everyone in the house would know what she knew. She suspected the ones most caught off guard would be her boys. She had a feeling their best friends, Cam's in-laws, had a good idea something was different—but special different—in both Jackie and their daughter-in-law from the very beginning. Tyler and Tommie conceded that they both felt their mom was special and their sister even more so. They now knew their niece would be even more special. Johnathan and Nivea took it all in stride. They had figured the Jackie and Cam part of the equation out years ago. The granddaughter portion of their explanation caught them a bit off guard.

* * * * *

As expected, Angela grew into a beautiful radiant woman. Her family watched as her knowledge and wisdom grew day by day. She was truly one of God's special people. As a teen, she participated in the institute from time to time. She was rarely challenged in public or private school. Her participation at the institute was more of a leader than a student or teacher. She moved from group to group spreading her knowledge, wisdom, and love to all who would listen. It became perfectly clear to Cam and Joseph and everyone else why Joseph and Cam had built the institute, although they did not know it at the time. The tremendous financial success of the Eagle's Nest Global Research Institute was now seen as possibly a source of money for Angela's and God's work to come.

On her eighteenth birthday, Angela called for a meeting in the original boardroom. She requested that all of her family be present.

"I am so thankful for you and love you all. The warmth you now feel running through your veins is the spirt of William and Martha McDonald. We are all here.

"You have given me everything I have needed decades before I was born. You all are special people whom God has richly rewarded. I must soon leave this farm and all of you. I will return to you every Christmas and share those special days with my family. When I am gone, my spirit will soar high above with the eagles watching over you. William and Martha can now go and enjoy their heavenly reward for the rest of eternity.

"Mom and Dad, within two years, I will marry. His name will be Jacob. He will take care of all my needs, if you know what I mean."

She looked at her mother and grandmother and smiled. Cam and Jackie returned a smile.

"He will be loving and kind. We will care more about each other than ourselves." Another smile.

"Jacob and I will give birth to one child, a girl. Her name will be Martha. Jacob and I will continue the mission that you both started. It will be Jacob's idea, and I will follow but lead, if you know what I mean."

This time, Billy, Joseph, and Johnathan returned the smile.

"We will build these institutes all over the globe. These institutes will deal with solving the problems of the sick, weak, hungry, and the poor. We will speak for those who have no voice.

"Martha will be the worthiest of all McDonald women. Millions and millions of people throughout the world will be drawn to her. She will spread God's love wherever she goes. Martha will be the last McDonald woman to carry God's torch. The McDonald family will continue to be blessed, but our mission will be accomplished in God's eyes. I thank you all for this farm. I know Eagle's Nest was part of God's plan from the very beginning."

They joined hands, and Angela continued, "May God bless William and Martha McDonald for their faith in God and their vision for Eagle's Nest. God bless this family, our friends, and Eagle's Nest. Amen. Adjourned."

# Epilogue

Cam, Joseph, Angela, and Jacob would oversee eighteen Eagle's Nest Global Research Institutes throughout the world, while Martha would spread God's love and wisdom worldwide. All five would be revered for their wisdom and love and have instant access to world leaders. The plight of many worldwide improved as the result of the research carried out in the eighteen global institutes. Global and regional conflicts disappeared during Martha's tenure. Cameron and Joseph followed Angela, Jacob, and Martha worldwide pursuing God's mission and helping complete the final stages of the McDonald family, its legacy.

# About the Author

Scott McKissock was born and raised in the small Northwestern Pennsylvania town of Cambridge Springs. He graduated from Edinboro University in 1973 with a bachelor's degree in biology and attained his master's degree in education from the same university.

Scott's childhood and early adult life was centered around athletics, participating in many different sports in his high school years at Cambridge Springs High School. Scott played college football at Edinboro University from 1969 through 1972. He was a member of the 1970 Edinboro championship Lambert Bowl team as a backup quarterback.

Scott spent the majority of his teaching career at Cambridge Springs High School and was revered for his enthusiasm and quality of teaching by his colleagues and students. He was nominated by his students on several occasions to *Who's Who in American Education*. He was inducted into the first class of the Cambridge Springs High School Athletic Hall of Fame. He always loved his job and looked forward to the day's learning with anticipation. His first four manuscripts were written between 2018 and 2021 (see author's note)—the first, *Eagles Nest*, followed by *Twisted, Madame President* and *McDonald and McDonald* to complete his *Billy and Jackie McDonald* series.

Printed in the USA
CPSIA information can be obtained
at www.ICGtesting.com
CBHW031606131124
17315CB00023B/357

9 798892 437257